[

bracket

[

First published in Great Britain in 2004 by Comma Press
www.commapress.co.uk
Distributed by Carcanet Press
www.carcanet.co.uk

A CIP catalogue record of this book is available from the British Library.

ISBN 1 85754 769 1
The publisher gratefully acknowledges assistance from the Arts Council of England
North West, and the Regional Arts Lottery Programme.

Set in Bembo by XL Publishing Services, Tiverton
Printed and bound in England by SRP Ltd, Exeter

Contents

No Introduction

The authors in this anthology need no introduction. Not for the usual reason, that they're household names, but the more exciting one that there's no reason why we *should* have heard of them. All of them are new writers, with no major published fiction behind them for us to know about. Their stories were selected from open submissions, after a general call to creative writing courses, workshop groups and individuals.

More importantly, the stories themselves need no introduction. Short stories don't. Neither their protagonists nor their small supporting casts need make our acquaintance. And how can they, there isn't time? Denied the far-reaching back-stories and the elaborate foregrounds of the novel, or the complex, unfinished history of any novel-like characterisation, the short story is left with a peculiarly modern demographic to pick from. As a genre, it is peopled almost exclusively with strangers, solitaries and self-exiles.

JL Borges acknowledged as much in his *Labyrinths* story, 'The Waiting'. In an unusually straightforward description of a man on the run, he offers us an archetype for the anonymous short story hero. We join the man taking refuge in an unfamiliar district of Buenos Aires after committing an unspecified crime. He assumes a false name and then simply waits… either for the unfamiliar to become familiar or for his avengers to catch up with him.

Weeks go by and the man rarely leaves his lodgings. On the rare occasions he does go out, Borges gives him a quirk which cracks an in-joke with us about the very nature of the short story, and its distinction from broader artistic canvases. Borges has him go to the cinema. Once there, the man never ventures further than the back row of seats and invariably leaves before the end of the feature. 'Unlike people who read novels,' Borges writes, 'he never saw himself as a character in a work of art.' Well he wouldn't, would he. He's a short story character:

unannounced, unexplained, untitled. The model of detachment. No one could be less like the grounded, all-things-to-all-men Everyman that hosts the average novel or film – Borges' 'works of art' – those disarming protagonists who make us feel at home and win us over, the way all Everymen do. Short story heroes hardly win themselves over. They discover little, confirm nothing, and never feel at home, even at home. Where the novel is a high-walled country retreat of an art-form – built for families, ensemble casts, and unfolding personal histories – the short story (or at least the modern short story) is a hotel room, occupied by that ubiquitous, urban oddity, the individual.

William Boyd has compared the distinction between novel fiction and short fiction with that between epic and lyric poetry. In as much as the lyric gives birth to the confessional somewhere in the twentieth century, I'd agree. The short story is entirely about the unheard voice offered up to the firmament: solitary, beyond the reach of companions, and unable to confide in anyone else. Which of the characters in the stories collected here successfully communicates with anyone else? From the girlfriend on suicide watch in Mario Petrucci's 'Cord', as trapped and alone as her desperate lover, to the news junky in Tom Palmer's 'Do Something Good', escaping his own life into a televised war.

Solitude, and the reality that no one's listening, makes the reader's eavesdropping all the more intimate. With solitude comes impunity, so many stories, like lyric poems, veer towards the confession – if not in the first-person narrative voice, then in the wider interaction between protagonist and reader. A stranger, after all, is the perfect person to confess to. GK Chesterton observes: 'In the perfect stranger we perceive man himself,' and as the reader is only passing, the protagonist shares his secrets. Like Chesterton's perfect stranger, he 'always talks about the most important things.'

It's no coincidence that the most traditional story here, David Lambert's 'Redemption', and at the other extreme, the most sci-fi, Penny Anderson's 'Help Me', both deal explicitly with confessions. In between, the more contemporary characters have to invent their own, secular ways of talking to themselves. The means devised constitute one of the genius conceits of the short story.

Sara Heitlinger's 'Black Box' takes its cue from a portable ECG machine, which patients wear for a normal working day while keeping an hourly activity diary. In this diary, a wearer voices things she wouldn't normally have occasion to – the ECG thus becoming muse, addressee and diary all in one. Zoe Lambert's hearing-impaired teenager, in 'Ramshackle', is even more private in her thoughts. Failing to fit in with school friends, she confides passively with her mobile phone, not answering the texts from her mother, merely reading them. It's not that short stories are the only artform where the protagonist confides in the reader, using diary-like devices. Novels often use them. It's just that, for the duration of these shorts, such expressions are *all* the protagonist has. Where a novel's hero eventually has to go out into the world, and *be* a novel's hero, a short story's character is, for the duration, bound up in the bower of themselves.

Sometimes it's the expression, rather than the absent addressee that's objectified. In Jaime Campbell's 'The Removal', a man 'composes' his message to an ex-girlfriend in the form of a mattress he delivers, by hand, to her front-door. In either case, the act of using a physical substitute to ape normal two-way communication echoes quite clearly the ode and lyric tradition of addressing the inanimate.

Not all the characters in this book find black boxes to put their thoughts in, but all are in some way isolated; either cut-off entirely or from the one person they most need to be in contact with – which is much the same thing. All of them are prose lyrics, written in the dark, spoken without hope of being heard, and some – like Maria Robert's climactic 'When Silence is the Only Thing we Leave Behind' – even aspire to the oral original of the lyric, song.

So hush now, listen up.

The Removal

Jaime Campbell

Skinny pushed on through the crowds, through the rain. The hair now lank to his face. His clothes now soaking. His body aching as he strained to lift the double mattress that little bit higher; stop it dragging the pavement, stop it mopping the ground like a sponge. He pushed on. A simple wire-frame, like a stick figure hunched over, blown around like newspaper yet carrying on, struggling through a wall of people who just wanted to get home, get dry. On his arm a tattoo, a fairground ride looping over his shoulder and down to circle the heart. The two of them inked in there together, he and her, front carriage on the tracks at the start of the climb.

Their first date together.

The image now etched into his skin, always a reminder of that first moment when the rush was up and the heart was pumping, when the blood just had to flow. Yet the memory was yellowing now, sepia in nostalgia as he pushed on, desperately trying to pick up the pace even though the soft-fruit muscles that hung from his arms were vibrating like television fuzz with the effort.

Straining.

Aching now but growing as he dragged the double mattress up over his head to stop it trailing the pavement, stop it mopping the ground. 17:38. The light now fading as he pushed on against the flow, pierced by the spokes of cheap umbrellas when people just wanted to get home and he had no defence. No shield or armour against a soft almond eye that slipped one more drop into the rain, a tear for their old mattress as he carried on, alone now against the flow.

Three steps behind splashed the little fat guy trying to keep up the pace. Sweating. Panting. A soft rubber ball splashing around in the wet as Skinny pushed on through the rain. Through the flow of people as if pushing through branches and he was short, Skinny's sidekick, his hairline waving the white flag in surrender over a shoe polish moustache that slid across his lip to compensate, 'It's fucking raining, why do you have to do this now?'

– But no response. Skinny had nothing left to say. His bone white face sunk deep into the shoulders, intent on looking forward, blank to the concern.

'It's pissing down.'

– Still nothing. No look, no shrug. Just a face of intent. Two wooden eyes locked straight ahead with the wrought iron refusal to listen.

'Fuck off then!'

And for a moment he stopped. Skinny's sidekick stopped dead and with a deep ceramic sigh he doubled over, halving himself in the street as if reaching down to give up.

Give in.

Catch a breath as Skinny carried on against the flow, carving out a stretch between them that shouted. That screamed. And deafened by the distance, the little guy had no option but to carry on. Those regretful rubber legs kicking, pushing against the tide, his face a frown of intent as he clawed back the gap on that bobbing, weaving mattress up ahead.

'Talk to me about this?'

– Still no response.

'C'mon, fucking talk to me...'

– And he knew he wasn't helping but just couldn't stop. He wanted to fix things. Make it all better somehow, this fist between two friends, this swelling anger.

'...OK then stop! Just fucking stop!'

And for a moment Skinny stopped. For a brief mirrored moment they stood there in the rain, the space between them spreading out like weeds and vines.

Just stood there, eyes locked and staring with violin stabs. Then Skinny, his memory like a projector re-spooling the scene, re-playing the moment when he caught them, his little fat friend and her. When the heart became just machinery and the realisation formed eyes, a face, a voice in which to speak.

Telling him how to defend.

To protect himself and carry this mattress on.

For a moment Skinny stopped, silent, eyes crunching between tightly closed lids. His mind on single track.

The little guy's point-of-view left fighting for a shot at the screen as Skinny scratched a sneer and turned his back to carry on. Lugging that damp, now useless, mattress along and up the street. His short, fat friend doused with sympathy, doused with remorse yet driven to keep up as Skinny turned a corner. Picking up the pace. Tightening his grip. The weight now heavier through soaking yet lifting it that little bit higher, his once soft-fruit muscles now drawing up blood, sucking in air, using every reserve to steal the strength needed and carry the mattress on through the rain. Through the flow and like a pinball he bounced off each and every one, racking up a score, his head playing a fanfare of bells and electronic whistles to drown out the feeling, to drown out the thoughts.

The hurt he was feeling. The need to do this now in spite of the desire. The wish to climb back into that carriage with her, their first date years before and start again from the moment they hit the first loop. The regret now burning holes through him but he pushed on. No shield or armour to protect himself against another tear for their mattress, another for their bed.

'We never did it on it.'

– As though that made it all right.

'She wouldn't, she still thought of you... Despite the...'

– And he dug the spade in deeper for another shot of dead earth.

But the rain drove Skinny forward and the sound it made, like applause, encouragement to push on.

To continue and he tried to run now. Sensing the finishing line. The chequered flag almost near and waving, his legs carried him on. Gripping the mattress. Arms like wire. Fingers like fuses ready to trip.

Aching now but unwilling to give in, he lifted that mattress higher, gripped it that much tighter as he turned the corner, almost there, his little fat friend rasping to stay close, stay near as they both aimed for the same single door ahead. A single red door much like any other.

Now a target.

Now a goal and he had to. He aimed for it and fired, propelling himself straight, an arrow shot to the centre, to the heart. Pounding now as he tried to run, his round rubber friend gulping air just short of the bends as he watched Skinny steal ahead.

Reaching the red door.

And still holding that mattress like a child saved from a fire Skinny turned to face his friend: 'Open it.'

And head now hung like a wounded bird, he did. As if ageing in breaths, he unlocked it as Skinny let go and the bed slumped like a corpse to the floor. His voice simply cracking as he plucked out the words, 'It's all yours', before turning to pour away as his friend hung mute by the door, looking up to her.

Looking up to the woman who stepped out over the mattress to see. To watch him turn and her eyes, once wooden to him, now welled up with rain. The heart from that carriage years ago now torn like paper, crushed into a ball as the two of them stood staring, hyena guilt laughing as Skinny poured away.

Five Miles Out

Sarah Tierney

Her cousins camp here every summer. They talk about it at Christmas when Cass and her family go to stay at their house in Oxford. Thomas and Charlotte, the two oldest cousins, argue about who swam the furthest out, or who jumped in from the highest rock. Cass listens to them wondering why her and Isabelle don't compete on things like that. They've never played games like skimming stones, or holding their breath underwater. On their holidays at the villa in France they sunbathe with their walkmans on, or pour over old copies of *Glamour* and *Heat* in the shade of the walnut tree.

Here it's all action as they put up tents, race to the sea, splash around in the rock pools and play Frisbee on the beach. Even the ground beneath them won't keep still. They're on a peninsula that juts out into the North Sea. The waves seem determined to wear it back, to force the campers onto secure land. Chunks of clay and grass tumble from the cliffs to the beach. There's a pillar of chalk in one of the coves; a tall skinny column circled by churned-up sea. Cass read in the visitor centre that it was attached to the land once, then the earth around it started to erode, creating a cave then finally just a pillar standing out there on its own.

Last Christmas, Louise, the quietest and youngest of their three cousins, gave her and Isabelle two flat chalk pebbles that she'd painted fishing boats on. She said they were paperweights, so Cass put hers on her homework desk. When Mum told her that she would be going camping with her cousins this year instead of having their usual family holiday in France, she dug it out from under her A4 folders and turned it over in her hands.

'Why don't you paint one for Isabelle while you're there?' Mum said with strained cheerfulness.

'She's already got one.'

'She might like another. You liked painting last year.'

'She's not going to need a paperweight in hospital,' Cass replied irritably. 'She's probably too weak to pick one up.'

'Don't be silly, Cassie,' Mum said briskly. 'Are you coming to see her tonight?'

'I've got homework,' Cass said unoriginally.

'Well, I'll tell her you'll be coming later in the week.'

'Whatever,' she mumbled and span back round on her chair to tidy the papers scattered over her desk.

Cass sits on her beach towel next to Louise, among the white pebbles. Louise is building a pile of them, each getting bigger from the size of a playing card up to that of a table tennis bat. She says she's going to do a Russian doll type design on them. Cass can't seem to find the right one for painting. A lot of them have holes like Swiss cheese, or they're brittle at the edges and flaking away. She thinks about painting a picture of a lump of Emmental on a holey pebble. It could be a kitchen paperweight for shopping lists and recipes. She puts it in the pocket of her shorts.

A bigger stone flies past, hitting Louise's tower of pebbles and knocking it over. 'Thomas,' Louise complains, without turning round.

Cass looks over her shoulder to see her oldest cousin grinning at them from his perch on a boulder in the shade of the chalk cliff. 'Are you coming round the rock pools with us?' he asks. 'We're collecting winkles.'

'Have your sandwiches first,' Aunty Chris commands. 'It's five past one already. Go and tell Charlotte we're eating now, Thomas.'

'Can't I have mine in a bit?' Thomas says. 'I'm not even hungry yet.'

'No you can't. We're all eating together on this holiday. We're not having people skipping meals.'

Cass feels Louise steal a sideways glance at her. She pretends to be looking for stones. Another one with a hole. She pockets it. Perhaps she could do it as a doughnut.

'Come on Louise and Cass. Lunchtime,' Aunty Chris calls.

Yes, we heard, Cass thinks, putting her flip-flops on and standing up. Aunty Chris passes her a packet of ready-salted and a brown roll on a plastic plate. 'There's salad in the box,' she says smiling.

Cass sits down on the picnic rug and takes a bite out of the sandwich, not bothering to look what's inside it first. Aunty Chris eventually turns away. At least Thomas and Charlotte have stopped watching her eat now. The first few days of the holiday, she'd felt like the family TV. They'd all gathered round her with their dinners balanced on their knees, glancing up from their plates to see what she was going to do next.

Cass feels like a swim after lunch. She's slippery with suntan lotion and her face is covered in a film of oil from the crisps. Aunty Chris is obsessed with the one hour rule though. She's convinced that they're all going to get cramp and drown if they don't let their food digest first.

'Is it always this hot when you come here?' she asks Charlotte who is looking out to sea through her binoculars. A few fishing boats are drifting beyond the cove. Much further out is the hazy outline of a ship.

'No, it usually rains non-stop for a week. You and Isabelle are dead lucky going to France every year.'

Cass suspects that Charlotte thinks that they're spoilt. She probably thinks that's why Isabelle got ill.

'I'd love to stay in a villa,' she is saying. 'I bet it's really luxurious.'

'It's boring there,' Cass says. 'We're not even near the sea. Can I have a look?' She trains the binoculars on the ship, then tries to follow the swoop of a gull across the bay. She scans along the beach, onto the steep wooden steps that lead to the path up to the cliff top. There's a boy descending slowly. He stops to wait for a woman following him and offers her his hand when she reaches the bigger drop at the bottom.

'Who's coming winkle farming?' Thomas walks around to where the girls are sat on their beach towels.

'Yes, off you go, all of you,' Aunty Chris says. 'Leave me in peace for a while. And don't get cut off by the tide.'

They set off along the beach, Charlotte carrying a bucket for the winkles. They're nearly at the water's edge when Cass realises she's still got the binoculars round her neck. She jogs back to Aunty Chris and notices the boy and his mother have sat down on the sandy part of the beach. He's about the same age as her, or maybe a bit older; Charlotte's age. She wonders whether she should have asked him if he wanted to come with them. When she turns back she sees him watching them through his own binoculars as they jump across the rock pools towards the edge of the cove.

It's about two hours till low tide and they have to wade rather than paddle through the caves that cut through the cliffs. Cass doesn't enjoy going thigh deep in cold water thick with black seaweed. You can't see what's beneath you and you have to watch where you're putting your hands; red jelly sea anemones stick to the sea-smoothed walls. Charlotte goes first, striding out into the channel. Cass hangs back till last and steps into a pool churned with sand. Thomas is splashing around ahead and the sound echoes back along the cavern through light the colour of dying grass. The sea has left a residue of green against the chalk rock which fades back to white above the tide line.

The water reaches her waist then starts to drop away until only her ankles splash towards the shelf of rock pools stretching between them and the sea. The cousins have separated, all intent on finding winkles to fill the bucket. She wonders whether Isabelle would like it here. She can't imagine her older sister getting excited about rock pools. Not since she got ill anyway. She'd peer into them trying to see her reflection. Maybe the warp of the unstill surface would straighten out her own distorted vision and let her see herself as she really is. She wouldn't make it through the caves though. Her spindly legs would get caught in seaweed and she wouldn't have the strength to free them. Or a wave would sweep her off her feet and carry her out to the open sea. Cass thinks Isabelle would probably be happy out there, floating on her back with no one to bother her, just seagulls screeching in the sky above.

When they return an hour later, the boy is gone but his mother is still sitting in the sun, a book resting in her hands. She keeps squinting along the beach in the opposite direction from where Cass and her cousins walked. The boy must be exploring the rocks that lead around the headland from the other side of the cove. They went that way yesterday – you can't get very far before the waves crash against the cliff and cut you off.

Just before the rock ledges are submerged in the sea, there's a cave that Thomas said he'd seen people swim through last year. Cass peered into its gloomy green archway; the water looked deep and cold and no light shone through from the other side. The cave carved deep into the chalk cliffs. Thomas said it leads into a cut-off cove that is visible if you look down from the lighthouse path. He and Charlotte talked about trying to swim through and Cass was relieved when they gave up on the idea and set off back to the beach.

The boy's mother is packing her towel and book into her bag.

She brushes sand from her sun dress and sets off across the pebbles towards the far side of the bay. She must be worried about him, Cass thinks. Then she notices the blue of his T-shirt; he's climbing through the rocks at the foot of the cliff. His mother slackens her pace. She sits and waits for him by the bottom of the steps.

On the first night at the campsite, Cass didn't go out when she woke in the darkness. She felt trapped in the sleeping bag, in the cotton room inside a canvas pyramid. She lay awake watching the morning light filtering through the orange canopy. It filled the tent with soft yellow light. At seven when she stepped out onto the dewed grass, the air was duller and colder than it was inside.

Tonight she can't stand to lie awake and begins the careful zipping and unzipping that eventually sees her outside in her trainers and tracksuit. Louise, cocooned in her sleeping bag, doesn't stir.

She can make out the shapes of the surrounding tents in the moonlight. Charlotte and Thomas sleep in a new black domed tent, but no giggles or whispers come from inside as she passes. Aunty Chris and Uncle Tony have a bigger tent, all angles and guide ropes, and a plastic window across the kitchen area which is rippling in the breeze.

Once her eyes have adjusted to the dark, she walks up the field to the concrete block which houses the showers and toilets. The light is on and insects have flocked inside. Dozens of daddy-longlegs pattern the white sinks. Moths sit motionless on the rough walls or warm themselves in the harsh glow of the strip lights. A slim orange slug slowly ventures across the floor.

Cass goes around the back to the washing-up sinks and the rubbish bins. They are the old fashioned metal kind with black plastic hexagonal lids. They smell ripe with food waste: curled vegetable peelings, crusted baked bean cans, greasy plastic bacon packets and used tea bags, swollen and set. There's a Tesco bag beside them, she can't make out the contents and gives it a little kick to see if it spills. She turns when she hears footsteps in the field. The boy from the beach is walking away from the tents, ignoring the lights of the toilets. He heads for the gate that takes you out of the campsite and onto the lighthouse path. She wonders whether he saw her as he skirted the lit-up block. He lifts the sling of rope holding the gate shut and pushes open a narrow gap to squeeze through. It creaks as it closes. He looks up towards the toilets when he hangs the rope back over the post but she's moved into the shadow of a wall. He pauses for a second then starts along the path.

She crosses the campsite and glimpses him just before the land starts to fall away. She climbs over the gate and drops with a soft thud onto the other side.

Isabelle went wandering at night. She'd creep down to the kitchen in the early hours. Cass doesn't know how long she'd been doing it before she heard the bedroom door pushing across the thick carpet and light footsteps padding down the stairs. She thought Isabelle must be getting a glass of water, but she was taking a long time to go about it. Cass fell asleep waiting to hear her return. The next night the same sounds woke her again, and the same long stretch of silence left her wondering what Isabelle was doing down there at three in the morning. She left the warmth of her duvet to go and find out. From the hallway she saw Isabelle staring into the fridge, her stark complexion lit up in the humming light. Cass watched as she picked up a cling-filmed plate containing leftover chicken and stuffing from the Sunday dinner. She looked at it for too long. Cass shuffled in the hallway and she turned around guiltily.

'What are you doing?' Cass asked.

Isabelle put the plate back and closed the fridge door. 'Nothing.'

'Can't you sleep?'

'I just came down to get some water.' She took a glass from the cabinet and walked over to the sink.

Cass thought she may as well get some water too, as she was here. They both gulped a full glass down, standing opposite each other, watching each other's reflections in the window.

Cass reaches the edge of the headland where long, thin fingers of eroding rock stretch out into the sea. The narrow pathways to the tips of the ridges are only safe for seabirds. To her right, the lighthouse flashes in a slow, hypnotic rhythm that doesn't feel like a warning. Further inland the chalk of the old lighthouse, crumbling and unsafe, has its own eerie glow in the moonlight.

The boy is nowhere to be seen. He must have gone down to the beach. Maybe he's going fishing, although he wasn't carrying a rod or a bucket. Or maybe he's a smuggler waiting for a silent boat to glide in with a cargo of drugs and whisky. She looks out to sea but no lights pierce the black water. She hears gulls calling, the break of waves against the shore far below, the wind hissing through the barley in the fields.

Maybe she ought to turn back, but she wants to know what he's doing. He's a nightwalker, like her, like Isabelle. She imagines her sister wandering the hospital corridors in her dressing gown and slippers. Tiptoeing past a dozing nurse. No, they'd make sure she couldn't do that in there. She'd be locked in her room and accompanied to the bathroom. Mum says they watch them hawk-eyed.

Cass should have been more watchful, more suspicious. She should have registered the warning signs. She pulls her arms around her waist for warmth and begins the steep descent to the sea.

She stops abruptly when she sees him waiting on the beach at the bottom of the steps.

'Why are you following me?' he asks. He's a Geordie and he sounds curious rather than angry.

She doesn't have an excuse ready. 'To see what you're doing.' The tide is not far out. She's conscious of it creeping up the shore a few metres behind him.

'What's it to you?' he says, blinking at her. He's shivering in his shorts and a long-sleeved T-shirt. He wears trainers without socks and a towel is slung over his shoulder.

She shrugs. Wonders whether she should apologise. 'So what are you doing?'

'Going swimming,' he says casually.

'In the dark?'

He nods and turns towards the sea. 'I'm going to swim through the cave.' He walks away along the beach, the pebbles crunching under his trainers.

Cass watches him until he reaches the edge of the cove and starts to splash through the rock pools. She jogs to catch up.

'Isn't it dangerous?'

'Not really. I'm a good swimmer.'

'Why don't you do it in the daytime?'

'I was going to but...' He seems to be searching for a reason. 'My mum would have worried. I doubt she'd let me.'

They have to paddle up to their knees to cross the rock pool. Cass rolls her trousers up but the sea is choppy and they get soaked anyway.

'You could get stuck or get hypothermia,' she says.

He stops and looks at her. 'Why are you following me again?'

'What if you don't come back,' Cass says. 'I'll have to call the coastguard and wake up your mum.'

'I will come back. It's not even that far.'

Cass stubs her toe and feels the saltwater sting. He waits for her but doesn't ask if she's okay. At the entrance to the cave, it's hard to tell where the sea ends and the air above it starts. She can hear the waves echoing from deep inside. The boy is taking off his trainers. He screws up his towel and T-shirt into a ball and wedges them between two rocks.

'I don't think you should do it,' Cass says.

He doesn't answer. He sits down among the slimy bed of seaweed on the limpet-covered rock and dangles his feet into the channel. He immediately lifts them out, the shock of the freezing water shows briefly on his determined face. Then he dips his toes in again, his breathing light and fast. Cass looks out to sea as if searching for help. The boy stares into the water beneath him. A wave drenches his legs and Cass steps back against the cliff. 'Is the tide still coming in?'

'No, it's turned.'

'Are you sure? What if the cave fills up with water. You won't be able to breathe.'

He starts to lower himself into the sea. Another powerful wave crashes through the channel and he struggles to steady himself. He looks up at her and she sees that he's afraid.

'It's too rough. You'll drown,' she says flatly.

He hesitates. A surge of water forces him back against the rock. He pulls himself out and stands shivering on the side. 'Maybe it is a bit rough,' he says quietly. 'I've still got tomorrow to do it.'

'Why do you have to do it at all?' she asks.

'Because I've decided I will,' he says. He's vigorously drying his arms and legs. 'I have to do it before I leave.'

She remembers Charlotte saying a similar thing about a rock she'd been daring herself to jump off into a deep, still inlet that they called the Mermaid's Pool. Cass and Louise had been content to loll in the cold water, feel the soft green seaweed between their toes. Charlotte climbed to the top of the overhanging rock and sat there for about half an hour trying to psyche herself up. Cass and Louise got bored and set off back. Charlotte caught up with them, still dry, looking annoyed.

The boy is holding onto the cliff, leaning into the mouth of the cave. 'There's a cove on the other side that you can't get to any other way,' he says over the sound of the sea. 'I bet no one's been there this summer.' He turns back to Cass then frowns. 'None of your gang have been through, have you?'

'No. Thomas and Charlotte talked about it then decided it was too dangerous.'

'Thomas and Charlotte,' he repeats, sounding a bit amused. 'They your brother and sister?'

'No. Anyway, I bet loads of people have done it. You're not going to be the first.'

'I'll be the first that I know about.'

The boy doesn't make to leave so she sets off on her own. She hears him following a few metres behind her all the way back to the campsite. Maybe walking away is always the best thing to do. Charlotte had given up on the jump once her audience had disappeared.

It didn't work like that with Isabelle though. Her obsession grew while their backs were turned, and tomorrow night the boy will probably try again. Cass hopes she will sleep right through for once. She wants to wake up in the morning to find him and his mum frying bacon and halved tomatoes over their gas stove. She wants to see him eating his breakfast peacefully, having swum through the cave and come back again.

The next day the sea is still and calm. The sky is almost cloudless and the warm, sweet smell of clovers swells along the lighthouse path. Cass lies on the grass looking over the cliff edge into the cut-off cove. Far below, the waves lap against a slim crescent of white stones. The air between swarms with gulls and kittiwakes. They perch in holes and ledges in the rock or circle on the currents over the blue sea. The racket from their startled, harsh calls breaks the peace of the farmland behind her. Occasionally one rises higher than the cliffs and is silhouetted against the ripe corn rather than the gentle waves.

They don't blink, she notices. That's why they always look so hungry. And yet they're meaty birds. Their feathers are sleek and well-oiled. Their wings look strong and their chests bulge. You could live off one for weeks. She wonders what gull tastes like. Fish and seaweed with a chalky residue, layers of fat to keep them warm in the gales.

Cass and Isabelle started dieting last summer, but as with most things,

Cass wasn't as good at it as Isabelle. Her sister had control and focus – she was conscientious about homework, would train hard for her swimming competitions. Cass tended to lose interest in hobbies and swap from one to the next. She'd forget about the diet for a few weeks, then seeing Isabelle looking skinnier, she would skip breakfast and lunch for a couple of days to try and catch up. Isabelle's hips were now jutting out in her swimming costume. Her forehead seemed bigger and her cheekbones more pronounced. Cass disliked eating in front of her. Isabelle pushed boiled potatoes and peas around her plate while Cass, starving, would shovel them in when she hoped her sister wasn't looking.

Soon though, Isabelle was absent completely from most meal times. She was out running or she'd gone to the swimming baths straight after school. With all this training she'd been doing, it was a surprise when Cass went with Mum and Dad to watch her race backstroke and whilst she usually came first or second, this time she finished last. But the real shock was when, floppy with exhaustion, Isabelle struggled to pull herself out of the pool. She fell back into the water and tried again, her embarrassed blush more obvious because her hair was scraped back under her swimming cap. Dad half stood, as if he wanted to go and help her. Mum's face was very still. Isabelle shakily lifted herself out of the water then hurried to the bench to wrap a towel around her. She wasn't quick enough, though, for them not to notice that a near skeleton had just climbed out of the pool.

Cass reluctantly gets to her feet and sets off back to the campsite. They're supposed to be going on a trip to Filey this afternoon. Tomorrow they're going to Scarborough to watch a battle re-enactment at the castle. She follows the path past the barley field and sees Aunty Chris waiting by the campsite gate. A mobile phone is held to her ear.

'Here she is, she's coming,' Cass hears her say. Aunty Chris beckons her to hurry up, then hands her the phone. 'It's your mum,' she says.

Cass takes the phone wishing she was still looking down from the cliff top. She feels sick in her stomach and unsteady, like a wave has swept away a chunk of her and washed it out to sea.

That night she waits for the boy on the beach by the steps. She's put an extra jumper on but it's warmer than yesterday. There's no breeze and the stars glow behind a thin layer of cloud. There's a light far out in the sea. It must be a ship or a fishing boat. She likes knowing that someone else is awake, even if they are separated by miles of cold, deep water.

She begins to think that maybe she's too late for him. That he's already swimming through darkness to the isolated cove. He turns up just when she's about to go back to the campsite.

'You waiting for me?' he says as he climbs down the steep steps. 'I've got a girlfriend at home, you know.'

'I don't fancy you.'

He jumps down onto the pebbles. 'Good, you're not my type.'

'You're not mine.'

'Come on then, if you're coming.' He sets off across the beach at a quick pace. She wonders whether he's rushing because he's worried that he'll lose his nerve again. 'Last night here. Last chance to do it,' he says.

'It's my last night as well,' she says. 'My dad's coming to collect me in the morning.'

He glances at her. 'Don't you want to go home or something?'

'My sister's in hospital. I've got to go and visit her.'

'What's wrong with her?'

'She's anorexic.'

They reach the part where you have to grip onto the cliffs and edge along the rocks.

'A girl at my school had that. She went proper skinny.'

'That's like my sister.'

'She'll start eating something soon,' he says confidently. 'The girl I knew got better after a few months.'

Cass doesn't say anything. They're at the entrance to the cave. The sea is very still tonight and she can hear the water dripping from the roof into the channel. The boy takes off his soaked trainers.

'How long do you think it will take?'

'I don't know. About ten minutes there maybe. Ten minutes back.'

She nods and looks at her watch.

'Why don't you swim it too?' he says.

'I thought you wanted to do it on your own. It wouldn't be as good if someone else did it with you.'

'You're right. It wouldn't.' He's jigging around with nervous energy. 'Okay. Now's the time.' He sits down, slides through the seaweed

into the water. 'Jesus Christ. It's freezing.' He treads water in the middle
of the channel then starts to swim towards the mouth of the cave.

'You don't have to do it, you know.'

'I do. I'm not backing out now.'

'Twenty minutes,' she says. She watches him swimming
smoothly into the darkness. The gloom swallows him after a while but
she can hear the gentle splash of his strokes cutting through the water.
Then there's nothing. She sits down on a rock covered in slippery green
seaweed. Out at sea the ship is moving across the horizon. She imagines
a sailor on board steering away from the pulse of the lighthouse above.

The last time she saw Isabelle her hair was falling out. It was the same
pale yellow as her complexion and she showed Cass how easily it came
free in her hands. The skin around her mouth was cracked and it bled
when she smiled. She'd lost one of her front teeth. She got out of the
bed and shakily walked around it to put a postcard in Cass's hands when
she could have just passed it to her. A nurse glared in through the
window on the door and gestured to her to lie down again. Isabelle
rolled her eyes – a truly horrific expression on someone as gaunt as her.

Cass didn't stay long. She'd timed it so that she arrived close to
four o'clock when the visitors have to leave while the patients have a
high calorie drink – an ordeal that takes at least an hour to get down.
There were about ten of them in there, all with that same alien look; big
head on a frail body, wide hungry eyes with a tight, cracked mouth. Cass
went to McDonald's on the way home then threw up in the woods
behind the house. She decided she wouldn't visit again. If Isabelle wanted
to see her, she'd have to start eating. She wrote her a letter saying as
much. At the last minute she squirted it with dewberry perfume – they'd
always claimed that the smell of it made them hungry.

Cass looks at her watch. He should have reached the other side by now.
She imagines him wading out of the cave onto the untouched pebbles.
The birds swooping and screeching around his head while unblinking
eyes stare down from the amphitheatre of white cliffs. He will be sitting
on the stones in this remote place, shivering and trying to summon up
the energy to swim back through the cave.

Twenty minutes pass. Then half an hour. On the phone earlier
Mum said that a doctor told Isabelle today that she's got about five days
to live if she doesn't start eating again. That's Friday then, Cass thought.

She would have been back home by then anyway but Mum said that Dad would collect her from the campsite tomorrow.

'You want me to come home so I can say goodbye,' Cass said.

'No, not to say goodbye,' Mum said firmly. 'You're telling her – we're all telling her – that she's got to start eating. If she sees us all together...'

'If the doctor couldn't persuade her...'

'She says she's thinking about it,' Mum said. 'I think she is. I think she's going to try.'

Out at sea, the ship's light has disappeared. She listens for the sound of him swimming back through the cave but she can't hear anything and it's been twice as long as he said.

Cass doesn't think Isabelle will have any more weekends. There's no sign of the boy and she's already waited too long. She leaves his towel and trainers by the mouth of the cave and sets off back along the rocks towards the beach.

An Obsession with Orange

Char March

They all say it suits me. Except her. She sits in her perfect skin. Shelling peas. Or bending. Weeding round the sweetcorn. Or transplanting tomato seedlings. Their heated green stink furring up our nostrils. And she says *How do you know it suits you? Maybe you're an Autumn.*

Does she want me in browns? A russet orange?

And she flips out the tiny silver notebook from the back pocket of her shorts. Above the rip where the curve of her beautiful backside slides into the muscle of her thigh. And she jots down the number of her Colour Therapist for me. Again.

And tomorrow I'll go out – again – in my lilac-blue. And she'll cluck with those most kissable lips. Raise her grey eyes to the sky. And I'll say *But I like it. I think it suits me.* Of course, I'm only holding out because I sense she wants me to. And it hooks us both into conversation – into a delightful sort of… tussle, almost. Although it's only a conversation of sorts – hardly bread and meat.

I decide to make a concession. I shall start shopping at Sainsbury's. After all, I don't want her thinking I'm a lost cause. Definitely not that. Yes, I shall swap the turquoise of Asda for the rather common orange of JS. It'll let her see what an influence she is on me. That I am listening. That I value her advice. That I want her to change me.

* * *

This is her apple. It's very brown now. I forgot about the power of lemon juice. Until today. And that's three days too late. This is where her teeth tracked through the flesh. Her squint front teeth that add that quirk to her laugh. That flash of unevenness in all that flawlessness. That glimmer of attainability.

I found it in the jungle garden that she is sculpting from the triangle of land stranded between the backs of our two houses. It is almost as if she is weaving this garden – from the extravagant trailing vines she has begged from local stately homes, from her exotic-coloured climbing beans, from fretted willow splices. And she has studded all this living weave with a miscellany of containers. Old boots, dolly-tubs, tyres and huge lopsided terracotta pots – her 'pottery-class mis-shapes' she calls them. And from these tumble black-eyed Suzies and Scottish flame flower, wild strawberries and swishing clumps of bamboo.

She has not bothered with a gate into the jungle. She is decidedly bold. A forwardness I find shocking – and delightful. She has simply knocked down the sandstone wall between the jungle triangle and her house's back garden. I watched her do it. She pinned me at my attic window, gazing down in awe. She came out swinging a sledgehammer like a croquet mallet. Backwards into her crushed-silk skirt and forwards with grunts of laughter. And a sudden squeal when one of the honey rocks bounded onto her sandalled foot.

I rushed for an ice-pack, arnica cream, Rescue Remedy. But when I arrived gasping at the emergency site, I found just the jumbled boulders of the tumbled boundary. Heard hearty voices coming from her kitchen. Left my offerings on a remaining tooth of wall. But found them today, the arnica tube already rusting.

And so, she has acquired the land. I like her acquisitiveness. I encourage her to borrow my brand-new gardening books – hope she keeps them.

So her house-garden now flows seamlessly into the jungle. But I know where the dividing line is – between the living weave of the common triangle, and her house's personal space. It is delicious – this wait, until she invites me to cross over. To sit across from her under her pergola. Under that wonderful mess of clematis and climbing roses. To walk through the heady swaying borders of rosemary and curry plant. I imagine their pungency drenching every crease of my lilac-blue clothes.

I was not a gardener until I met her. Had to buy books, spend hours and hours pouring over them – to identify all the things she so easily names. All these plants she casually trails through her fingers, chats about as if they are... another aspect of her. As comfortable as her clothes.

But the jungle is, I feel, common land. Neither hers, nor mine – I like to think of it as 'ours'. A beautiful word, for a beautiful place.

To get into the jungle, I have to squeeze through the rotting plank fence at the bottom of my back-yard – for mine can't be called a garden. There is nothing in it but the two bins, the climbing frame (still in bits) and all the oddments of plastic furniture that have never been comfortable – no matter how many cushions you stuff them with. I am ashamed of it all. It'll have to go. And the scabbed tarmac with its lush dandelion patch. I plan an assault on the Yellow Pages – there will be a helpful man with a pneumatic digger who also happens to grow the most wonderful herbs... Even, perhaps, ones she hasn't got. There must be some type of startling orange mint or orange lavender or something. I shall present her with a huge aromatic bouquet.

★ ★ ★

Marmalade. Yes, it's clear that the swap to Sainsbury's will not be enough. Not enough of a sign, a signal, to her. So, until the Yellow Pages herbman comes through, I shall make her marmalade. I shall start tomorrow. The sting of zest is already in the air. For I shall do fine-cut; and thick-cut laced with an Islay single malt; and a gallon or so perfumed with elderflower blossom because I read that elderflower marmalade is just like sealing up jars of summer air. And this summer – our summer – is so special that we will want to have at least some of it for later. In gleaming jars sitting on our shelves. But these extra additives must not affect the colour. It must all be as bright as Belisha beacons. Each fat jar a startling neon. Luminous in the sauna of my kitchen; the whole house sweating with the effort. I'll start at dawn.

She'd been called inside by the phone. To a friend. To a child. Perhaps to a husband. And her apple was left – rocking slightly. Like me. In the wind of her passing. I brought it in. To sit on my table. It is here again now – in the lamplight with me. Blue night is leaning against all the windows. The house ticks. Finally relaxing its grip on the heat of the day. I have slit the plastic sheeting from the sofa, found a pillow. The radio burbles 'Sailing By'.

I set it rocking again. By the steam of my coffee. By my sticky pasta plate, my emptied salad bowl – for I have to keep my strength up. I have a reason now, after all.

★ ★ ★

I am fierce in my gentle holding of her as she tracks through my flesh.

She leaves her unmissable mark. Then takes my hand. A stream of bubbles giggles from her mouth. Her teeth flash against the background sway of seaweed. She is holding up a skein of red silk. It flows around her. Puckering round her nipples. Slipping between her legs. Slowly I shake my head. My hair swishes in slow motion tendrils above my head. The red is now yellow. A rich butter that highlights the gold of her skin. Lights under her chin. I swim towards her. Reaching for the light.

There are bells. A mass of tones and patterns. You can hear the weight of them swinging. Feel the stones of the belltower creak with each pull of the fat and furry ropes.

I'm face down in the dribbled pillow and *Today's peel was from Howden Minster in East Yorkshire.* Then they're straight into Drumcree and the screeching Orange Men, their drums battering Catholic ears, and then on into parliamentary sleaze stories. I am a tousled splotchy-white wreck from a night underwater. I stumble to the bathroom. Fumble with a toothbrush. Drag back the curtains. Peer out. And there she is. Swinging. In the jungle's hammock. Caught in the very early morning sun. Barefoot. One leg dangling. A Victorian nightdress. High collared. Long-sleeved. White. And even ironed. Her hair is down. I've never seen it down before. Its silver-grey waves reach thickly to mid back. She is reading. One arm behind her head. She has half-moon glasses on. An intent expression.

I drop down. Crouch, behind the half-height lace curtain. Then peer out again. Expecting her – and the garden – to have vanished. Helena's Midnight Garden. But there it is – there she is. Swinging. On the ground is a crumpled eiderdown. Old and patched with faded silks. On it sits Orlando. My cat. Bastard. How dare he be keeping her all to himself.

I grab a comb. Haul on shorts – blue – while still gobbing toothpaste. Then my best shirt. Lilac. And espadrilles. Purple.

Stepping out, their rope sucks up the heavy silver of the dew. Goosebumps crop my arms. My toes are clammy. *How can she lie there in a nightie?*

I turn back. Haul a fleece – mauve – from the jumble of coats. Silently close the back door. Tiptoe-tread to the gap in the fence. Take two deep breaths. Try to think about Chi. Realise I look suspicious. Snatch up a bucket. A trowel. And swing into the jungle. The greens are luminous in the 6am light. Tender and limp. They unload their weights of thick dew as I push past. Drench me with chill. I try to whistle a nonchalant tune. Head down. Pretending to spot seeding docks, dandelion clocks, rogue landcress. I round the big pear tree. And she's gone.

Orlando gently swings in the hammock. Half-sitting. On a huge velvet cushion that's losing its stuffing. Kneading it with his claws. Tilted in the grass underneath, her teacup. Inside, a seeping cut of lemon. Dregs of Lady Grey. A cigarette butt. Half-drowned.

All cold.

I cradle each in my palms. Tenderly take out the stub. Place it between my lips, close my eyes and press. Her tea dribbles out, over my chin, drips into my fleece.

I shall plant nasturtiums. I've heard they're easy to grow. Don't need much looking after. Like poor soil. Those trailing ones that grow like Triffids. They'll cover the tarmac, the dandelions, the wheelie bins, the house, in no time. And impressive blooms. That orange you can barely believe. One of the books tells me you can eat them – the blossoms and the leaves. Tangy, like acidy watercress – it says. I could present her with a bowlful. She likes salads. I saw her eating one yesterday. She could have my flowers in her salad every day.

Love.

I try it out in my mind. It flickers. Elusive. Insubstantial. I gulp coffee – to oil my rusted-shut tongue. It hasn't tried this word for four years now. I barely whisper.

I love her.

It sounds huge in my kitchen.

I stand on the back step. Face the jungle. The sun is now starting to pour over the roof of my house, to rub the shoulders of hers. Splashing itself into her bedroom window. Open. Filmy cream curtain flapping lethargically.

I stand in the shadow of my house and say it.

I love you.

Three binmen suddenly tumble round the corner whistling. Solid skirts of black bin liners swag-swaying against their orange cotton bodies. More Orange Men. It is a sign. A definite – and wonderful – sign. They are followed by the bleating reverse of the lorry. And its terrible breath.

My husband blunders in. He bumps his way over and around the boxes – they are all over the kitchen floor. I have not attempted to unpack. He is trying to button his cuffs. He is asking where the toaster is; is there any bread then?; what about milk?; am I sure I'm okay?; did I not hear Jamie crying in the night? He is saying that he'd come down in the early hours, found me, but couldn't wake me; that he's got a big meeting this morning and can't find a decent shirt; that Miranda wants to go swimming today; that she says I left them both at the nursery again yesterday, but surely I didn't?; that he knows I'm tired, but so is he. Then he stretches over the stacked cardboard minefield; turns my face gently – very gently – towards him; holds my passivity in his palms; looks worried; is worried; has every right to be worried, I suppose; kisses me; gets no response; sees the clock; starts to speak again; stops; grabs the car keys; tries out a big smile; how about a meal out tonight?; he'll ask at work if someone can recommend somewhere nice around here; how about Thai?; see you later, sweetheart, okay?; see if you can find the toaster.

The Volvo takes him away. I reach for the phone. The nursery can take them both again. They'll even pick them up. I go back out – walking steadily towards the gap in the fence.

I have known her for five days. five whole days. The rest of my life stretches out before us.

The Priest

Tim Cooke

There's someone on the stairs again, the bloke from downstairs, The Priest, playing his pan pipe. I'm stuck in the black lift of my depression as always, falling through the floors with dizzying speed, but I edge out along the hallway anyway, parting the darkness as I go, and look through the spyhole to make sure it's him. He's not visible but there's something about the random, automatic quality of the playing, the pointlessness of it, that tells me it's him. As I crouch down and listen to the squealing mess of sound pressing under the door, I feel, not for the first time, as if I am under attack.

A week ago he was out on the estate cursing at three in the morning:
'Your fucking IRA, your CIA, your CID, your tenants' association, your fucking middle-class urban decay junkies, your cat-lovers, I fucking hate you all, you cunting tourists.'
The tirade went on for two hours during which he managed to castigate, with some originality, almost the nameable itself. Two years ago I would have gone down and had a word with him, talked him out of it, laid a reassuring arm upon his shoulder, but now that I have lost my mind, now that buying a pint of milk is near the limit of my capability, all I can do is listen, mortuarised in bed, staring at the cracked and faded white of the ceiling, and wait for his psychosis to burn itself out. My worst fear as the list mushroomed beyond plausibility was that there was method to it, that it was a form of divining and that he was seeking amongst his lexicon for the source of all his pain and anger, his true enemy. I found myself mouthing the words for which he was searching and thinking with mounting horror that I had reached them only a second ahead of him and that as soon as they were reiterated by his own lips he would turn to the window and then hurtle up the stairs and hammer on the door, the awful crowd of his madness streaming behind him.

But the moment passed and the multiplication of paranoias was averted. In fact the final object of his derision was a yoghurt pot he found attached to his trousers after falling off the stolen car parking sign upon which he'd been precariously balancing. This I observed guiltily, my chin pressed to the window-sill, before watching him disappear through the door directly beneath me. There was the slurring of feet, then nothing. The sign swung unsteadily for a few moments more, seeming briefly almost animate against the dark grass, then as if suddenly reacquainted with its own futility, ground abruptly to a halt. In the distance I could hear the Mancunian Way and Princess Parkway across the mouldering rooftops and it sounded like bliss.

Some days I don't hear a peep out of him. True, there is the stench as I pass by his door, which I guess counts as some sort of contact, and always some new graffiti or scrawling, the latest being, improbably, a backstage door sticker for a girl band called the Sugababes. This level of interaction suits me fine. Then there's just me to deal with, dragging my lifeless form through the dreary rooms of my first-floor mausoleum where months can go by without a single object moving apart from the two plates, cutlery and mug that shuttle between the living room and the washing-up bowl. Everything is exactly as it was two years ago, as if I had died back then and have been living on in memory only. The dust is that thick, all the plants are dead, and the walls are hung with shabby items of clothing from more glorious times. Two years ago I thought I had completely lost my self. Now I realise that I have lost even that loss. In such a situation, when you can no longer see the big picture because you are no longer part of it, details are everything, details are all there is left.

Two years ago nothing happened. Nothing really anyway. My housemate left, returned to Vancouver. True, he felt like a soul-mate and losing him was like letting go of the best part of myself, but at the time I felt quite powerful, magus-like, and we had fallen out somewhat and I thought it would be best for both of us. But what moves in when the best part of yourself moves out? Can a man die because he loses a friend? Looking at the minutiae of the situation, the detail that strikes me is that he took my guitar cord instead of his, mine with the brand-name Piranha clearly marked in white on black rather than his own which had no label. Did he do that out of affection, because he wanted something to remember me by? No, because he already had several more appropriate items. Or was it a simple mistake: he just grabbed the wrong cord in the hurry to get packed? Unlikely, he was very precious about all of his music gear. So why? What did the cord signify? I stared blankly out of the window at the grey, morbid sky that seemed to hang permanently over Hulme Park in the unlikely hope of finding inspiration or solace.

The cord connected my Fender bass to its Trace Elliot amplifier. So did it earth me, ground me in some way? Was it my connection that he took, that he coveted and wanted for himself? Who was he anyway, this Canadian who appeared from nowhere and moved into this flat within a few days of me arriving myself? Who became so quickly such a close friend, whose music sounded from the first so delightful, so natural, so perfect, as if I had heard it all before? More than that, I thought with a start, as if I had written it myself, as if it was somehow my music too. From the stairwell, as if by way of sardonic commentary, a guitar started to strum tunelessly. The Priest. Fuck. That meant I was imprisoned for the next couple of hours unless I fancied trying to get past him on the stairs. This was no easy task since The Priest always sprawled across the landing effectively barricading the way and moved to block you if you tried to go around him. At the same time he would be staring with unseeing eyes at some insignificant scrap of nothingness on the wall and acting for all the world as if he were in some sort of deep trance or meditation rendering him incapable of speech or understanding. Whether this was a real manifestation of his illness, a consequence of his medication, or an affectation, I didn't know. Maybe it was all three. But it was certainly unnerving, the sort of challenge that you didn't need when your head was fit to explode with self-doubt and foreboding and you were having problems going to the shops.

I turned on the TV and tried to drown out the sound but he had started singing now and it was impossible not to listen. I was fairly sure that he just made the lyrics up as he went along – they certainly never sounded as if they'd been crafted in any way or honed to work with a consistent theme or even with each other. It was just the cursing in the night by other means as far as I was concerned. One of his favourite tricks was to repeat the same word over and over again whilst playing a two or three chord sequence. Today the word seemed like it was 'dislocation'. This could go on for an hour without the slightest variation, following which there might be a slight shift in emphasis to something like 'I'm dislocating' or a verbal pun such as 'in dis location'. It was agonising, especially to me since he seemed to have precisely the ability to be in the present that I lacked. For whilst it's true that I sat in my flat and, generally speaking, did nothing because my brain was so messed up that I couldn't work or socialise or even read, this was more because I was so overwhelmed by the total fuck-up that was my past and the anxiety that this generated than because of anything actually happening in the present or likely to happen in the future. My mind seemed to have ganged up on itself and was in the process of eradicating any connection that it had with reality, even with itself. Shit, there was that word again – connection. Wait. Hougen had taken my connection because I was so intent on losing it myself, because he was sick of it, wanted me to see what I was doing to myself. My better half took my connection with reality because he was that connection i.e. he effectively took himself!

I stood up and started pacing around the room, my head in my hands, my eyes darting between the dilapidated mismatched sofas, the wooden pallet covered in badly arranged bits and pieces – candle-holders without candles, empty room fragrance bottles, a stripey sausage-dog face down in the dirt – the browning remains of the dragon tree in the corner, the numerous worn-out pairs of shoes on the floor. Incoherent fragments, shards of a life, signifiers of ruin. I went over to the mirror and gazed desperately at the face I no longer recognised as mine.

The Priest was really getting going now. The words had changed and I strained to hear them. I'm always nervous of going to the door because I'm sure either that he can hear me, or that his psychosis grants him supernatural powers and he can sense my encroachment, my presence, my auditory voyeurism. So I stood by the door to the lounge and inclined my ear in his direction. He was doing an exaggerated Radiohead impression with plenty of phlegm and the mantra he was cycling through like Thom Yorke on opium was:

'You're disconnected, yeah, you're disconnected.'

Everything in its right place. Maybe there were no accidents, everything was scripted, all the world a stage, though not a divine authority but instead a sort of evil genius. Or perhaps you oscillated between the two like a pendulum, divine authority / evil genius according to some sort of magnetic orientation, the way you were facing at the time. Look down and all you see is hell, look up and there's only heaven. I began to get a very bad feeling about The Priest. I had lost faith in Hougen, that was the truth of it, I had stopped believing in him. I thought I could survive without him. As a result, he had left and taken my guitar cord with him and since then I had been falling non-stop, indeed I no longer felt like I existed. A reasonable period of time had been allowed to elapse and then The Priest had arrived. The black lift I was travelling in had stopped at his floor and he had got in.

A distorted version of Hougen, like a reflection in a trick-mirror at a fairground, he looked like a movie-maker's idea of an asylum inmate. Shaved head, glaucous unfocused eyes, twisted grin, pasty dough-like skin, menacing mien and clothing presumably from a skip – though he was undoubtedly capable of intelligent thought he concealed it well. Where Hougen was musically adept and generally astute, the only reasoned communication I had had with The Priest was when he knocked at my door and asked me if I could teach him scales on the piano. Where I had welcomed Hougen into my flat and given him a room for two years, loving his genial sort of madness, I squirmed away from any contact with The Priest, telling him that I was too fucked up, too doped with anti-depressants to teach anyone anything. Since then we had nodded at each other a few times, grunted to say hello but our communications have been strictly early man. For months now I have seen him as nothing more than a nuisance, an irritation that I can't scratch, an encumbrance like a scab or a tumour that has attached itself to my block of flats. Most of the time I have not looked, I have ignored, I have stepped over and passed by but for someone so confined, I should have realised that there is more at stake in such a person coming to live in my block. I should have seen him in relation to Hougen. I should have put him in context. I should have seen him as a motivated sign and not been taken in by the apparent Brownian motion of his behaviour.

I went into the kitchen and started the kettle boiling to make a coffee, realising that it was two hours since I'd started my reverie about Hougen. The Priest was humming now, much quieter, stroking the guitar as if he was gradually passing out. Sometimes when he stopped playing he just lay there, which meant you never knew for sure whether he was still on the stairs or not until you opened the door. It seemed like he was heading that way now. I wondered who he actually was. Where he came from. Why he was called The Priest, for fuck's sake? Though things with him had begun slowly, in the colon as it were, the recent metastatic proliferation made it difficult to understand why I had never asked any of these questions before? Why was I so scrupulously not interested in him? It began to look like a psychological strategy, not so much repression but more what I remembered Freud calling 'foreclosure', treating something as if it did not exist, a technique reserved for true horrors. But how could I find out more about him? I looked in the fridge and found that I'd run out of milk. 'Screw your courage to the sticking point', I thought. There was no avoiding it - I would have to go out.

The boiling of the kettle had momentarily drowned out the sounds from the hallway and now as I listened I realised they had completely died away. Gone or comatose, I had to find out. Putting on my coat, I eased the door open a crack and gingerly stuck my head out. There was no sign of him. I shut the door behind me, locked it and made my way towards the stairs feeling as if clouds had suddenly given way to clear sky. True, he may be waiting at his door to loom out at me as he often did, but I could brush my way past that with a cursory 'hiya'. I hurried down, intent on getting out of the building as quickly as I could, determined not to give his doorway even a glance, but as I passed it by I sensed that something was not quite right and looked around. I had evidently felt a draught or some sort of emptiness emanating from the flat, because when I turned I saw that there was no door in the doorway. It had completely disappeared. More madness, I thought. He's removed his own door in an attempt to get back to an even more primal stage of development. I pulled back, imagining him coming at me with a club, clothed in animal skins, his face camouflaged with excrement. For a second I fancied I saw him in the darkness but it was just my own mind projecting ahead, plaguing me once again.

More to quell my own fear than out of curiosity or concern, I called out:
        'Priest? Priest? Are you in there?'

The words span into the mouth of the flat like stones, ricocheting harshly. But though the darkness seemed to have a voice and certainly possessed quite an odour, neither were sufficient to make me believe the flat currently contained anything particularly animate and, without really knowing what I was doing, somehow impelled by the situation, I found myself crossing the threshold. I tried the light switch. Nothing. No bulb or no power. I took another step, or rather slid along like a cadaver entering a furnace. I knew the layout of the flat – it was the mirror of mine so all I had to do was think in reverse. Down at the bottom of the hallway was the sitting room. That's where I would head first. Now that I was in there, in the guts of his abode and with a legitimate excuse, I was intrigued as to what I might find. Perhaps I could answer some of the questions, find out who he really was, what he was about. I knew I might not have much time, so I made the lounge as quickly as I could, stumbling over unseen debris, and scraped down the wall where I knew the light switch ought to be. It was there, and this time the light came on, although it was a red bulb and made me feel as if my eyes had suddenly switched to infrared.

I looked around me, swivelled my eyes here and there, trying to pick up some information quickly. The floor was carpeted with clothes; I had felt that with my feet but now I could see them, dozens of garments but no actual carpet beneath them, just cold concrete. To the left there was an old and seemingly melted computer, like something out of Dali, every part of it seemed to be burned and mis-shapen. Grotesque though it was, it was the same model as my own, an Apple, so he had had taste – and money – once. By the side of it there was a stack of handwritten sheets, a book of some sort perhaps since I found it hard to believe he could still be a student. However the top sheet had the word 'shit' scrawled across it in what looked like blood or something worse. By the window there was a television or what remained of one: the tube was smashed and a broom handle was sticking out of it. To the right there was an immense mound of objects that, out of the corner of my eye, in the darkness, made me think of cows piled up, a great pyre. Books, and beneath them records – singles and albums. Masses of them. I bent down and picked up a handful of paperbacks. In the gloom I could just make out the covers and some of the titles: 'The Nature of Things', 'Seven Clues to the Origins of Life', 'The Postcard', 'Four Fundamental Concepts'. I started slightly, somewhat bemused. These were all books that I'd read, that I'd once possessed. I grabbed another handful: Barthes' 'S/Z', a Haruki Murakami, 'The Theory and Practice of Hypnotism', an A to Z of Brighton. Ridiculous, these were all mine too – and much more unlikely. I fell onto my knees and ploughed into the barrow, hunting for vinyl now: The Pale Saints, Slowdive, Dif Juz, Bauhaus, a staggeringly rare Joseph K single. Every time my hand came up, it was with a record or a book that I had not only once known but that had previously been mine. Crazy. I delved again and again but there were no exceptions. Not a single aberration from that rule, and I searched and I searched through what must have been well over a thousand objects, tumbling the mountain down around me.

By the end I was drained, almost diseased, and felt like I was losing my mind all over again. It was impossible but there it was. All of the precious belongings that a bitter ex-girlfriend had once given away to charity because I hadn't been able to pick them up on an allotted day, they were all here. In The Priest's flat. The whole of my book and vinyl collection built up over thirty years. What, had she given them all somehow directly to him? Were these actually my things, or was this just some sort of carbon copy of my own unique journey, a continuation across dimensions of a chaotic logic? I scrabbled around to see if I could find an inscription, a name in any of the frontispieces or on the sleeves but came up with nothing. They probably weren't mine then, I thought, slightly relieved, but that didn't make the situation much better. Was I really supposed to believe that The Priest had read all of those texts? Tracked down all of those singles and EPs? That he had, by himself, without aid of any kind, built up such an esoteric collection? That he was that sort of guy? But then I'd amassed them in the first place, and what sort of a guy was I now?

I realised I had to get out of there. I was losing my grip and if he walked in now I didn't think I could cope, would probably just scream – which might lead to anything. But as I left I couldn't prevent myself from glancing quickly into the bedroom – my bed, the same make, a Panasonic hi-fi, ditto – and the kitchen – an old Moffat stove like mine – enough to realise that The Priest's flat was like a hellish vision of my own, maybe ten years down the line, that he in some sense was me, that the universe was mocking me once again, playing a sick joke on my naivety, balancing out some sort of dreadful equation for my benefit. I wasn't who I thought I was. No one was. We were all just parts of something, heads on a single, bifurcated body, bound together by the same deep structure that could show you the good side or the bad side of itself depending on the decisions you made, the people you loved, the people you rejected, the direction you took. I knew which side I was being shown and I felt like Scrooge after the vision of Christmas future, only truly damned.

When I got back into my own flat I slammed the door, locked it and then slid down it onto the floor. If The Priest was me, or some part or version of me, and he'd been moved into these flats because of his relation to me, then who was everyone else? Carlos on the top floor, Elaine, Michelle downstairs, Thomas opposite? The only one I ever talked to now was Thomas and even he'd stopped borrowing tobacco like he used to or giving me plants, and talked to me in that patronising, slow way people use for those they believe have lost it. I realised that over the past two years I'd stopped talking to everyone on the estate, many of whom I used to count as friends. If they are all part of me, if I am somehow living inside my own mind, then I am becoming a particle in an environment that abhors the particulate, a single neurone disconnected from the net. Suddenly, behind me, underneath the door, I hear what sounds like a dog sniffing.

I jump up, startled. A dog? Then I realise that the dog is enunciating something: not quite words, but not animal sounds either. A grinding, guttural monotone. Horrified, I run into the bedroom and shut the door. I turn on the light but the bulb explodes and the darkness caves in around me and something like dynamite goes off inside my head. I am panicking badly, have to control my breathing. If all the people in this block are in some sense here for me, feel me, sense my disconnection from them, then what about everyone on the estate? This peculiar, road-locked, ramshackle, paralysed estate on the shoreline of the city centre? Is this why I beached up here? A place that is literally at the end of all roads? What will happen now that I have seen the books, the records, the flat, now that I realise what is going on?

I grope my way towards the window, desperate for air, and look out onto the avenue. At first I think that something has happened to the grass below, that it has become somehow lumpen, goose-fleshed, horripilated but then gradually like a magic-eye picture I resolve the image. There are hundreds of people standing on the grass, in the darkness, staring up at me. The strange effect is made by all their heads together so unexpectedly. Their eyes glitter dully like felspar in granite. I blink in refusal, cast about wildly for the car parking sign only to find that it has disappeared, swallowed up by the heave of bodies whose mute ceremony slowly forces itself upon me. It is incredible. From the numbers it appears that the whole of the estate has turned out for reasons that both appal and are beyond me, and as I stand transfixed I have the vertiginous sensation that the floor beneath me, the very earth, is slipping away. Such a crowd, such a mass. So many people I have ignored and let slip by. But where is he? Where is The Priest? Behind me there is the click of the door opening. I half-turn. The black lift has stopped at the basement, and they are waiting for me to get out.

3,000 Degrees

Fiona Ritchie Walker

Churches. They've got a smell all of their own. I could close my eyes and know instantly where I was. Not that I spend a lot of time in them. Up until a few months ago, I couldn't even tell you the last time I was in this place.

Mind you, today's visit was planned. Katie and I booked the date for our wedding over a year ago. But I was expecting to be waiting in this vestry, with Neil, my oldest mate, as my best man. Only things didn't work out like we thought. And since my last visit here, I've been thinking about the soul. You know, what happens after we die. Because Neil is dead. There, I've said it. He died. Didn't pass away. I didn't lose him. He died.

Last time I was in this church was for his funeral. Neil and me, we'd been friends since we started school. Scouts, the junior football team - you name it. Even when we left school and Neil went to university while I started work, we were still great mates.

Of course, when Neil graduated the job offers started coming in. He could have gone to the States, but he stayed here, in Newcastle, where his friends and family are.

We were never apart for more than a few days in all those years, which is why it was such a shock. One day Neil was out clubbing with us, cracking jokes, planning a weekend away for my stag night. Next day all over. Not even thirty.

It was my Katie that found him. She'd gone to Neil's to pick up some disk and take it into the office. Something about the internet connection being down so he couldn't send an important document that was needed straight away. She set off dead early, wanting to miss the worst of the traffic. Anyway, the next I knew was a frantic call on my mobile. She'd got to the flat to discover Neil in bed, not moving. What should she do?

Of course, she'd already dialled 999 and the ambulance was on its way. I was stuck in traffic heading in the opposite direction. By the time I reached the flat, no-one was there.

None of us could believe it. Neil's parents took it really badly. I found myself dropping in after work for a cup of tea. I'd spent half my childhood growing up in their house, slept over so many times. I needed to know they were OK. I think it helped them too, us talking about Neil, the things we used to get up to.

One evening, I could see that Ann, his mam, was on edge. I was just about to leave when she stopped in the doorway.

'Al, I wonder if you'd do us a favour. We should have done it sooner, checked on the flat, but neither George or I can face it and I just wondered…'

Getting out of the lift, it took me right back to the first time I'd been there.

'So, what do you think, Al?'

I remember walking round, my voice echoing in the empty space. 'I'm impressed. Bit of a step up from where you are now. And that is what I call a bathroom, Neil.'

He grinned. 'Power shower for the morning. Spa bath for those romantic evenings. And a nice big bedroom too.' Then I noticed the view.

'No more brick walls to look out at, eh?' he said. 'The quayside is something else and this place, it'll be my pension plan.'

'Katie would do her nut for a view like that,' I said. 'Can you afford it?'

Neil rubbed his chin and smiled. 'Heard on the grapevine that the owner's desperate for a quick sale. It's a risk, me putting in an offer before I've even got my place on the market. But what the hell, this place is a bargain that won't come twice.'

'What about furnishing it?' I said, always the practical one. 'Can't see your stuff looking good in here.'

'White wood, simple lines. That's what this place needs. And some cream curtains in the lounge, right through maybe, not those patterned things that are up now. Katie said she could run me up some for half the shop price.'

His words hit me. 'Katie? Has she been here?'

'Don't be daft. Would I ask anyone else to see it before you?'

'So how come Katie's offering to make curtains for the place?'

We were walking to the front door. Neil turned and punched me on the shoulder.

'Because I had to book a time to view and she is my PA. A damn good one.'

How could I forget. That's how Katie and I met. I rang to speak to Neil and she wouldn't put me through. I thought she was a right cow – until I had to meet Neil at work and saw this good-looking girl at the desk. How wrong can you be? When I rang Neil, Katie and I would have a bit of a chat. After a while, I discovered I didn't like it when I got straight through to him – I missed that beautiful voice.

I plucked up the courage to ask her out – couldn't believe it when she said yes. I was over the moon when she agreed to move in with me, and then after about a year, it seemed us getting married would be the next step. So we fixed a date.

Katie's really the practical one you know, a great organiser. The files she's kept on the wedding. That's why she's such a good PA. She was a real help to Neil's folks when they were organising the funeral. They appreciated all she did, but it was me they came to when they couldn't bring themselves to collect Neil's ashes and scatter them. So what could I do? I had to say yes, which was why I ended up taking a day off work and heading to the crematorium.

I thought people's remains might come in something a bit more... reverent – know what I mean? Not a dull brown, plastic screw-top jar. I couldn't put Neil in the boot, so I propped him up in the passenger's seat next to me. Like old times. Don't know why, but waiting for the lights to change, I just... opened the jar. Dug my fingers in. Weird. Like a coarse grit. And I started wondering if Neil could feel my fingers running through his crumbled bones.

And then, I suddenly found I wasn't driving out of the city anymore. I was turning back towards the river, towards Neil's flat. I could feel his front door key in my pocket and I knew exactly what I was going to do.

'Here we go, Neil. One last visit home. You and me,' I said, walking in with the urn under my arm. I put Neil on a table and went to put on some music.

'What were you listening to that last night? I know you, couldn't live without music. Oasis? Oh. Wrong there. Just shows how much I know. Madonna.' I picked up the CD cover. 'Madonna? Since when did you listen to that crap? I know, you were probably working on some promotion. Looking for a backing track, that'll be it. So, let's get rid of that and find some decent music.'

I put on Oasis and started reliving the past, remembering me and Neil in the front row. Just us and that wall of sound and light. We were wet as if we'd been swimming when we got out. Freezing cold by the time we reached the car and our ears ringing like we'd never be able to hear properly again.

I found a beer in the kitchen, opened it and drank a last drink with my old mate. Then I started wandering round the flat, remembering times when we'd been there, some of the daft things we'd done, until I ended up in the bedroom.

'So this is where it all happened, Neil. You got into that bed, set the alarm, switched off the light and never woke up again. Maybe you'd just read a few pages of that book. Halfway through… Makes you wonder how long any of us have got.'

And then – I'm not proud of this, mind – I found myself looking through the bedside cupboard.

'Very responsible, Neil. Ribbed for extra pleasure. The girls must've loved you. I'm surprised they're not flavoured. Vibrator too. Wonder if that was Katrina's. I thought things might have been getting serious between you two, but she didn't even play the grieving ex-girlfriend at your funeral. Never even turned up. You never did tell me if her suspicions about you seeing someone else were true.'

And then I found this box, right at the back. Opened it up and discovered some serious jewellery. A ring with diamonds that put Katie's engagement ring well in the shade. I put it back in the drawer and went back to the living room.

Neil and I ended up watching the football on TV. Me on the settee, him propped up against a cushion. I unscrewed the jar, like it would make a difference, like he could hear the commentary. Maybe it was the drink, but I liked to think that he could hear every glorious minute as Newcastle won through to the next round of the cup.

When I left the flat I put Neil's ashes in the boot, promised myself I'd scatter them the next weekend. And I really meant to. But it was raining on the Saturday, so instead, I took him down to South Shields. Parked at Trow Quarry, ate some fish and chips, just like we used to.

I told him about the new CDs I fancied getting and how I'd missed out on promotion. Again. I told him that his mam and dad had announced they were going to give his flat to Katie and me.

Katie had been stunned when I broke the news. 'A wedding present? What kind of people give the flat their son died in as a wedding present?'

'Katie, it's a two-year-old flat in one of the most sought-after locations in Newcastle,' I said. 'I know Neil died there, but it wasn't like he was murdered. And if we don't take the flat, we'll kick ourselves one day. Do you have any idea how much it's gone up by since it was built? Neil had it for less than a year and it's worth £40,000 more than he paid for it.'

'Fine. So we ask them to sell it and give us the money. Or we sell it. That would work.'

I shook my head. 'No, no it wouldn't. Maybe in a few years when we've got kids.'

Katie thumped her coffee mug on the table. 'If, Al. If we've got kids. I don't want to even think about a family until I've got that promotion to office manager and made the job mine. At least *I* want a career.'

There was a long pause. 'OK, then,' I said. 'If we have kids we could think about selling. It'd be natural. We'd need the extra space, a proper garden, but until then…'

'I don't want to sleep in that room.' Katie's bottom lip started to quiver. 'You didn't see him lying there. You don't have the memories.'

'We could move things around,' I suggested. 'I could make that a study, put the computer in there. We could get rid of all that bedroom furniture. Come on, Katie. Give it a go?'

Eventually, she nodded. I knew what she meant though. The more weeks went by, the more I found myself missing Neil in the strangest places. Like my kitchen. I started remembering all the times I'd come home and Neil had been propping up the breakfast bar, a beer in his hand, while Katie was busy cooking. I remembered the days he gave her a lift home from work or came round to drop things off.

I wondered if it would feel strange when we moved into Neil's flat. Katie, on the other hand, seemed to be becoming more enthusiastic at the thought of the move. She'd set off for the flat with a notebook, tape measure and shade cards and I could see she was enjoying making plans. The wedding was getting closer too, making her even more busy.

One Thursday we went late night shopping at the Metro Centre so she could look for clothes for the honeymoon. She was in one of the changing rooms and had given me her bag to look after when her phone went off. It was hopeless trying to get it out and I lost the call, ended up dropping the bag on the floor. And then I saw it. Suddenly my hand was in the bag, taking out the box, opening it. And there it was. The same ring. Couldn't be two like that.

Katie's phone started to ring again. This time, a text message and I was on automatic pilot, picking up the phone, opening the message. Nothing special, just some deal if she topped up her pay as you go account, but then my fingers were pressing the messages button and I was looking down the list. My own message from the day before, and another one kept. One that I opened. One from a number that I recognised. 'When r u going 2 tell him? 8 as usual.'

And I suddenly thought of Katie, the super efficient PA, wanting to avoid the traffic jams, so helpful whenever her boss's email wasn't working, and it being no problem for her to pop over and pick up things to take into the office. And I started wondering what time she got to work. Then I remembered the ringtone on her phone. Madonna.

And just when all of this was going through my head, and I was still kneeling on the floor with Katie's bag between my knees and that diamond ring glinting in its box, Katie came out of the changing room. I put the ring away and acted like nothing had happened.

There's a lot you learn about people over the years. Katie takes a size 10. She drinks coffee but hates tea. Her favourite film is *When Harry Met Sally*. Her ring finger is the same size as my pinky.

It's not that I set out to know that, just that when I bought her engagement ring, the one we'd chosen together, I took it out of the box, wondered exactly when I'd give it to her. And I held it up to the light, watched the blue and the gold sparkle, then tried it on my own hand, and found it fitted my little finger. As if it had been made for it.

The day I discovered Neil's ring in her bag, after we'd gone to bed, I just couldn't sleep. I lay there wondering and eventually I had to get up, walk through the dark into the living room, find her bag, and the box, open it up and try on the ring. Found it fitted my little finger. As if it had been made for her.

I lay on the settee, the orange from the streetlight making strange shadows around me, and I thought I saw Neil sitting in his favourite seat in the corner, a beer balanced on his knee, until I looked carefully and saw it was my coat thrown over the back.

'Listen, Katie, you went to Sunday school, didn't you?' It was the next day and we were both in the living room.

'Yes…' she said, with a puzzled look on her face.

'Well, you know we're all supposed to have a soul. So, does everything leave the body when we die?'

'How would I know?'

'I was just thinking… Suppose something stayed in the body when life ended.'

Katie shook her head. 'You've been watching too many late-night horror films.'

'Well, when a friend dies, it makes you wonder. What happens? What if you touched Neil's bones and somehow… he knew?'

'Knew what?' Katie said.

'You know… He might recognise the touch of someone's fingers. The way that if I was asleep in bed and felt you caress the back of my neck and my shoulders – not that you've done that for a long time – but if you were to do that… those long, delicate fingers stroking my skin, I'd know instantly that it was you.' I felt her body stiffen. 'Think if you ran your fingers through Neil's ashes he'd have that same sweet feeling of recognition? What do you think Katie?' And when she started to cry, I knew I'd found my answer.

Everyone likes Katie. She's so generous and caring. I remember Neil telling me he just couldn't manage without her. Told me I'd no idea how talented she was. She's super-efficient too. I found a note on the fridge door marked *Al – check weather forecast, scatter ashes.*

I started to think back to the way she kept checking to find out what I was doing, where I was, when I'd be home. I remembered the way Katie was so sympathetic when Neil and Katrina split up. How she invited him over at Christmas when she knew I was working, saying it was better for the two of them to be watching the telly together than on their own.

Katie's note about scattering the ashes kept bothering me. I planned to do it that weekend, but on the Friday, in the canteen, I picked up a newspaper. Started flicking through, killing time until the other lads came down. And this story caught my eye. Made me think, Neil, this is for you. So I picked up the phone, found the company's number and made a call. Booked him in for a blast of 3,000 degrees Celsius.

The timing worked out well, what with me and Katie getting married today. Three years we've been together. It's not always been easy. I thought she might want to call it off, what with Neil going to be best man, but when she realised it meant such a lot to me, we went ahead with it.

Maybe she realised, who knows what might happen in the future? What might be round the corner. Know what I mean? Maybe she's decided that life's too short and we've got to make the most of what we've got. And she's got me. Oh, no, I'd never leave her, she knows that now.

It's almost time for our wedding. Katie will be arriving any minute and I've got something really special for my bride. 3,000 degrees... That's some heat, isn't it Neil? Bet you never thought you'd end up in a jewellery box. Amazing... the way heat can transform burnt bones into diamonds. Every woman's best friend. And what, with that ring in your bedroom drawer that just happened to be the perfect fit for my Katie's finger, I think diamonds are something that both of you found special.

I had these beauties made into a ring for Katie. Didn't want you to completely miss out on the occasion, did I Neil? And me? Well, I wanted my own little keepsake. We've been through so much together... shared so many things...

So I booked myself into the dentist this morning. Still feels a little strange, having a diamond stud in my front tooth. But I'll get used to it. Oh yes, Neil. I'll get used to having you around. Wait until you see what I've got lined up for me and Katie tonight. The honeymoon suite. Champagne on ice. Soft music and candlelight. Katie in one of those silky numbers that suit her so well. I'm sure you know what I mean, Neil – and how she likes to be kissed all over.

You and me Neil. We'll be revisiting all those warm, familiar places. Let's get ready to kiss the bride.

Black Box

Sara Heitlinger

I am in your clinic this morning at ten o'clock. I have been out of the country and I suspect I've caught some exotic heart disease. You make me take off my shirt and bra and you take a swab of cotton wool and wipe cool liquid across my chest. You dip your hand into a box full of rectangular pieces of Scotch Bright, pull one out and scratch it across my skin so that the surface of my body will accept the stickiness of five white, round electrodes: two for my left breast, two for my right, and one above my right breast. (If they are here to monitor my heartbeat then why are there more on my right side than my left?) The electrodes are connected, via five tangled wires, to what vaguely resembles a regular, black walkman. You inform me that my heartbeat is going to be recorded for the next twenty-four hours. The tape will be listened to and analysed and in ten days time I can pick up the results. I didn't know they make cassettes that last for twenty-four hours. You say: 'This one lasts much longer, but it moves much slower.' It's true: you push *Play*, and before you put the walkman into a pouch and tie it around my waist, I look down at the cassette and see the spokes are barely moving. After I put on my T-shirt, all I can see of my new bionic apparatus is an unfashionable black pouch. I've never worn one of those before. 'Keep your bra on tonight,' you say before I leave. 'And fill this in,' you add, handing me a folded piece of paper.

I leave your clinic with your five fingers on my pulse. They're making my acquaintance. They're recording my every move like paranoid security surveillance. Nice to have you here, make yourself at home. I hope you enjoy your stay. I hope you find me fascinating and fall in love with me and won't want to leave. I'll have to rip you away from me in any case. I have to live my life, you know. I can't have you here forever.

Pacing the polished marble floors, I make my way to the *Exit* sign in the building where your clinic is housed. I feel like I'm floating in a bubble world. I recall an afternoon I spent in London. It was a hot day during a hot summer and I was walking the streets in a thunderstorm with a portable compact disc player. I had taken it from the Whitechapel library, I had to leave my passport as a deposit, and I was listening to the voice of a Canadian woman who led me through the streets of East London in a strange, atmospheric film-noir-type murder mystery. While I walked in the rain I heard sounds – people talking, music, traffic, footsteps, horns, trains – and I wasn't sure if they were noises from the real world or from the CD: I'd turn around expecting to see an oncoming car and the road would be empty; I'd hear people chattering from inside a shop I was approaching, but when I got there it would be closed. Now, again, there's an audio device hanging from me, and I can't work out why, if this time I'm being recorded, everything feels so unreal.

Outside, I sit down on some stairs and take a closer look at the piece of paper you gave me. It is inscribed with the words, *Activity Diary*. Under this is written, 'In order to compare the recorded ECG chart to the actual activity that is conducted, you are requested to carry with you this activity diary and to record in it the hour, the type of activity and the accompanying sensation. The aim of the test is to follow the activity of your heart during your day-to-day activity: at rest, at work, while driving, while walking, during sexual activity and while eating. Remember! The more detail you provide of your activities and the sensations you have, the more assistance this will be for the doctor treating you.'

The initial discomfort wears off. I'm no longer aware of the physical feeling of the electrodes under my bra. But I have a strange hyper-awareness of what I am thinking, and of the world around me. I've been turned on. Nothing escapes me: I notice the flapping sleeve of the woman at a cash machine, cigarette butts on the ground, the dirty stone buildings around me and drivers with angry faces beeping their horns and filling the air with undifferentiated drones. I am cheered by a ginger cat trailing between the tyres of parked cars; a wall of garish underwear confronting the street crowd without inhibition makes me feel exultant. The machine is monitoring me and I'm happy. Keeping it all nice and slow. So slow it's barely moving. I'm happy because I've often dreamt of something like this, a machine that would record my every thought, twenty-four hours a day, so that nothing would be lost, everything would be captured. I'll ask if I can keep the tape. I'll want it for my grandchildren, or for my lover. I'll make those dear to me listen to it, sit them down and put them through it, so that I can be rest assured they know me intimately. Of course, I know they won't be interested – you're the only one who is. You'll learn things about me no one else can know: not my parents, not any psychologist, not my lover. You're the only one who will make the effort. I feel immense gratitude.

You want detail in my activity diary? Here goes. I'll give you pages.

1:00pm: At the market. I buy a kebab (my first since arriving back in the country) and sit on the curb. I throw bits and pieces of food into the street. Did my heart race? Was there any irregularity to mark my minor criminal act? I throw my paper bag on the ground. How about now? Nothing? Six months ago you may have felt something. I've changed after six months in developing countries where everyone throws their rubbish into the street. Are you shocked? And did you gauge the pleasure of eating the tender chicken after being vegetarian for so long?

1:30pm: I climb 17 steep stone steps at number 17 Sentori Street. When I reach the top my heart is beating fast and hard. The friend I have come to visit is not home so I sit down and listen. Can you hear that, my devoted listener? Can you feel it beating like a moth in a jar? Are you impressed now? Am I truly unique?

1:45pm: I'm approaching home. A woman outside a cafe is handling something, pushing her face up to it. At first I think she's cooing into her baby's face, but then I see it's a book. Book, baby.

I walk on. An elderly man is standing on the corner of my street preaching to an invisible audience. He is wearing a suit and wielding a prayer book. He looks like his heart isn't into it. I don't stop to hear what he has to say. I don't stay.

2:00pm: I'm twenty metres from home, and I'm resting, for your information. I'm thinking how come you're so sure I'll be back with your walkman tomorrow? There must be uses for a walkman that fits a one hour cassette into twenty-four. Or twenty-four hours into one. Perhaps it's just the thing I've been looking for. Do you really believe that people with heart problems wouldn't steal? In London I had to get my passport back, but what do I need from you? For you to tell me I'm healthy or ill? I'll be disappointed if you say there's nothing wrong with me. I'd rather have the heart problem. I'd like the gravity of that to get things into their right perspective. To kick-start me into truly living the life I was destined to live, compelling me to endow each moment with the weight it deserves, and invigorating me into taking nothing for granted. In other words, to stop me piss-farting my life away. So maybe it's best to leave things up in the air and to keep the recording going.

2:15pm: Don't be alarmed, I'm just walking now, opening the front door, getting a glass of water, opening the fridge. It's slow again, isn't it? I'm barely moving. Activity: eating an apple. Accompanying sensation: shivers up my spine. I feel my beat erratic, I sing my body electric.

3:00pm: You claim to want all my day-to-day activities. Don't say you didn't ask for it. Let's see what you think of this. Positively thumping, right? Can you guess what I'm doing? I'm not *doing* anything. I'm resting on the couch in the garden, not moving a hair on my head. That's not entirely accurate because I am doing something in a cognitive sense. I'm remembering certain things that happened to me. Certain things that make me afraid, that I don't like to think of, but that may shed some light.

My memory is this: I'm taking a flight from Bangkok to New Delhi on an ultra-modern aircraft. I don't like to fly. I can't help feeling helplessly out of control of my life when I fly. The idea of fate offers me no consolation. If I could fly the plane myself I'd be much happier about the whole thing. At least if I'm responsible for crashing and dying I'll have no one else to blame, and that puts me at ease. This flight, in any case, looks promising: there are private video screens in front of every seat; the wings curve upwards as if they're proud of their new technology; the air-hostesses look like sweet, girlie manga characters; the duty free range is crisp and modern.

I am sitting in a window seat overlooking one of the happy wings. Twenty minutes before we land, it gets very dark, very quickly. The menacing sky begins to make me uneasy. A flash fills up the sky and I know it's lightning but I tell myself it was just the sun peeking through the clouds momentarily. I can't afford to have seen lightning. Because if these are storm clouds and that was lightning, and we're airborne in a metallic vehicle, then we're going to die. A few minutes later I see lightning hit the wing of the plane just outside my window. The sky lights up and there is an explosion. People in the plane yell out. I find my hands in my mouth and my breath doing a sharp intake, but straight away I am aware that we are not dead, that the plane is not nose-diving and the only real danger now is that my heart is beating like a lunatic in my chest, throwing itself against my ribcage as though it wanted nothing more than to crash out of there.

Whenever this memory peeks through, my heart goes berserk again, as you can hear for yourself. I can play with it. The stronger I focus on it, the faster my heart beats. It's like sliding a blade of grass along an electric fence, feeling the pulse grow stronger until you can no longer stand it.

4:00pm: I'm going to have an afternoon nap now. Don't expect there to be much activity for a while.

4:15pm: Your presence is too new. I can't sleep knowing you're here with me; for me. So I've raised myself to light a candle and tell you of the sounds I hear from my bed. Outside, from across the road, is the loud, incessant, badly-timed ranting of a tabla drum. I rage that my neighbour suffers from severe arrhythmia and yet they insist on playing. For a while I consider going across the road to ask them to be quiet. But I lie here fuming instead, alone with you. How does severe annoyance register in my pulse?

They've become quiet. Now all I can hear outside is the wind in the trees, the wind picking up dry leaves off the ground, spinning them around and letting them go again. Inside my room, next to my head, I can hear the metronomic crunching of woodworms inside my bedside table, munching through nutritious wood, gaining sustenance and paving ways for future use and posterity. Two weeks ago there was only one worm. Now there are at least three. I wonder if one day the table will be such a maze of tunnels that there won't be enough solid to keep it together, and it will collapse into a heap of sawdust on the floor near my head. Would it still be a table? If not, then when did it cease to be one? Is something similar happening to me? Is there a tropical worm tunnelling through my heart?

8:30pm: If you can feel a strong beat now it's only because I have music going and I'm doing the washing up enthusiastically. I've finished the plates and cups and as I look down into the sink all that's left amongst the soapy remains of the passing week's meals is a random scattering of knives, forks, teaspoons, tablespoons, as well as the occasional chopstick, a wooden spoon or two, fluorescent yellow salad servers, a garlic crusher and a chic plastic vegetable peeler. Everyone's down there in the sink, absorbed with their petty issues, coexisting in slimy muck: knifes and forks are pairing up and separating; teaspoons are crying and demanding attention; tablespoons, forever androgynous, are acting responsibly; the garlic crusher is grumpy again. But when push comes to shove, each one of them wants, urgently, to be chosen, to be scrubbed clean, rinsed off and put into the drying rack. There's nothing they wouldn't do to be next in line.

With the soapy sponge in my left hand, my right delves down and picks up… the garlic crusher. I did it on purpose, and against my natural inclinations. What I really wanted was to clean the knives first, they were up there on the top of the pile, and with two sharp swipes they're clean. But I won't let them do it to me, I won't let them do it to the others. The old and sick, the needy come first. I stoically push my hand into the debris and, against my instincts, despite my disgust, make sanitary those utensils which I would prefer to have left till last. It's a matter of conditioning. If I overcome the way I've been conditioned to act with the little things, I'll be better equipped to deal with the big. I continue until all the cutlery is lying clean on the marble above the sink, my shackles left behind to rot inside. OK, that's enough excitement for now. I'll turn the music off and sit down again.

11:45pm: I've told my lover that you need to hear my heartbeat during all my day-to-day activities. Including those of a sexual nature. I explain it's for my health. We crawl into bed and wrap the blankets around our cold bodies. I am naked apart from the black pouch above my pubic hairs and the wires creeping up my torso like a vine, the electrodes like flowers bursting on my breasts. I am also wearing a bra, as duty dictates. My lover is non-artificially naked. He remembers a scene from a movie in which the awe-inspiring villainess, who has chopped off her own arm and is wearing a prosthesis, is about to fuck the hero before she kills him. She is naked apart from the harness that keeps her appendage in place. Straddling him, she says 'With, or without?' He chooses without. He's going all the way. I too sit astride my lover, bizarre medical apparatus entwining my ambivalent body, and I say 'With, or without?' We both burst out laughing, a little nervously.

We kiss tentatively, treading water before diving in. His hands stroke my body, I feel the softness of his skin come in contact with the plastic wires, rolling them against my skin. Laughter erupts from out of us every so often. I bend down over him and the pouch with the recording machine drops like a weight onto his belly. I push it to the side, cackle hysterically and then force myself to be silent. It's like we've got this kinky new toy and we're shy to use it, or there's someone else in the room watching us. We're embarrassed, and worried what it might mean if we let ourselves become serious and begin to like it. The giggling is becoming quieter, shorter and less frequent. Reluctantly, we let go of our embarrassment, like of an anchor that's keeping us from careening into unknown seas, where we don't know what might become of us and what we might become. We may not find our way back again. I open my eyes, expecting to see him still smiling. He's not.

120 beats per minute.

My laughter stops.

8:30am: I wake up after a restful, dreamless sleep.

At 9:30am I remove the electrodes. They are stuck firmly to my chest and I rip them off painfully. Sticky, grey circumferences of five circles are left as a souvenir. I place the whole spindly contraption into a plastic bag and walk unaccompanied and unaided to your clinic. I climb the stairs and see your door is wide open so I go inside. I hand you the plastic bag with the twenty-four hour sample of my heartbeat inside. On the desk in front of you five or six of the black recording machines are lying open, the cassettes nestled inside, like mechanical aliens in incubation awaiting your kiss of life.

What I Did On My Holidays

Emma Unsworth

Day 1

'Serbia?' he said. It seemed as though he'd said it twenty times now. 'Serbia?'

She'd woken with the taste of defeat in her mouth, to the sound of her phone ringing, to the sight of swallows flitting past the balcony. Early morning and an older man. Regret.

'Isn't there still a war on there or something?'

She allowed him to continue.

'I mean, I don't want to sound, you know, predictable.'

She drew a breath, paused, exhaled. Something stirred in the bedroom.

'Well, where are you staying for a start?'

'With a friend I met last night. There's no need to make a noise like that, Stuart.'

'So you got a package deal after all.'

Really it was the right time for a speech, to tell him exactly the way she'd been feeling, why she'd left, but they'd run out of speeches months ago. Now their conversations were distilled right down to bitter little witticisms that were, quite perversely, more impressive.

Something fell out of bed.

'Look, I've got to go,' she said. 'Do you know how much this costs?'

'Take care of yourself, Shirl.'

The phone went blank. She turned it off.

Šuki staggered out from the bedroom, his head huge and heavy looking. He wasn't wearing pyjamas. He stood in the middle of the small living room, the tatty books and gatefold records lying open like dead birds around his feet.

'English men work too hard,' he said. It makes them irritable. Coffee?'

'Yes please.'

He went into the kitchen, and she heard the sounds of porcelain on wood, of metal on glass, of glass on glass.

Šuki was a 38-year-old producer at the National Theatre, Belgrade. He shared a flat in a communist high rise with his sister Ljudmila, who was down in Montenegro for the holidays. The night before, Shirley had been glad to meet him. With his head shaved clean she'd noticed him right away on the bench outside the bar. He was wearing a cowboy shirt and she'd thought momentarily – stupidly – that he was American. As it turned out he was originally from Sarajevo, and quite a dancer.

She went into the bedroom to gather her things. A holdall, a denim jacket, some vodka and cigarettes in a duty free carrier bag. She pulled on her boots, listening to the groan of the lift, a big sad old sigh from the other side of the block. She'd listened to it all night.

'You want it in there?'

'No, I'll come through.'

Šuki placed two cups and an ashtray on the table. The coffee was strong and heavily sugared, barely liquid.

'Hvala,' she said, and he laughed.

'U redu je.'

There was a scab on the tip of his nose, a scarlet point that she couldn't help but watch as he finished his coffee and poured out some more.

'Ach, just mud.'

Saturated coffee grains chugged into the cup.

Out through the open window swallows flew, their forked tails dark and sharp against the sky.

Day 2

'So let me get this straight. You've gone to Serbia and you don't know when you'll be back. You know if you wanted to just break up with Stuart you could have done that in England…'

'It's not that simple, Sophie. And we haven't broken up.'

Shirley shifted in her seat. The bus to Zrenjanin was hot and airless. Sweat trickled down her calves.

'I still think you're nuts. Shirley fucking Valentine.'

'Sophie, will you do me a favour please? Will you let everyone else know so I don't get any more phone calls.'

'Why don't you just not answer your phone?'

'What if it's an emergency?'

'Turn your phone off then. That way you'll never know.'

'I need it for the clock and stuff.'

'Okay.'

'Will you?'

'Okay.'

Shirley put her phone away. The bus passed through a village, where dusty paths and forgotten gardens dissolved before her eyes. A cat slouched under a parked car. All of the cars were old, many French.

The girl sitting next to Shirley turned to her and said:

'Where in America are you from?'

'Oh no no, I'm English. Manchester. North.'

'And what do you think of Serbia?' the girl asked, waving a thin arm towards the window.

'Ooh, it's a bit hot for me,' said Shirley, flapping her hand in front of her face. 'But otherwise very nice.'

'I have never been to England,' said the girl, who had a huge, bright green watermelon balanced on her tiny lap. 'But I would like to go. It is not easy, you know, for us now. We must apply for papers. It takes many weeks.'

'Your English is excellent.'

'Thank you. I watch a lot of American… How do you say you know, *serious*?'

'*Series*.'

'*Series*,' nodding her head, 'I watch a lot of American series. They don't put the voices over the top, they have the words at the bottom. It makes it better for learning, you know. You hear how it sounds. *Friends, Simpsons, E.R. Simpsons* is my favourite. So funny…'

The girl erupted into laughter. Her voice came from right at the back of her throat, like a gargle. Shirley relaxed a little.

'Do you know the best place to stay in Zrenjanin?' she asked. 'I don't have much money, but I can afford a cheap hotel.'

As they were getting off the bus, Gagga carried Shirley's extra bag, the one with the cowboy shirt in it. A present. They were mad for presents.

Day 3

'Look, Mum, I'm not depressed. No, I haven't left my job. No, we haven't broken up. Well, that was a bad day. Everyone has bad days. You've had bad days. Yes you have. What about that time... Well, everyone cries now and then. It's healthy. It's like your body's water cycle, it keeps everything moving round you know, nothing gets stagnant... No, it's not every day. Well he's lying. She's lying too. Mum, I have to go now. Well maybe I am going to cry. So fucking what?'

Shirley pressed the little red phone on the keypad. She huffed a few times and hugged herself. There was a knock on the bedroom door. Shirley didn't make a sound. After a few minutes, she made her way over to the door and very carefully opened it.

There was a cup of coffee on the floor just outside the door.

'Hvala,' Shirley shouted down the hall.

Gagga came out of the kitchen. She was wearing a black and gold summer dress.

'My parents would very much like to meet to you,' she said. 'They are at my granny's in the next block. They have made food, if you'd like some?'

'Yes please,' said Shirley.

After coffee they walked across to the next tower block. In the concrete square, old women sat on benches, whispering and nodding, while children played football in the dried mud. Shirley avoided the women's eyes, she looked at their black clothes, at the football spraying up clouds of dirt as it bounced.

'You are quite an event,' said Gagga. 'Nothing ever happens in Zrenjanin. No one comes.'

The lift in the next block felt flimsy as it carried them up to the ninth floor. The Cyrillic graffiti on the walls looked like pictures. Gagga opened the stiff little lift door and said:

'After you, Shirley-girl.'

Granny had dyed red hair and a face as pale as milk. She pulled out a chair for Shirley and then poured her some rakija from an old Pepsi bottle.

'You want brandy?' Gagga asked.

'Sure,' said Shirley. 'That's plenty, thank you.'

She drank it down; as it hit her stomach she realised how hungry she was. Gagga's mother came out of the kitchen carrying a tray.

She came over to Shirley and kissed her cheeks.

'Eat,' she said. 'Please.'

The food was a kind of pie, leaves of pastry layered with ground meat. Gagga's father came out of the kitchen with a bowl of bright relish. He put it on the table.

'Paprikas,' he said. 'Try. Please.'

Then he went over to a chair by the window and lit a pipe.

'They don't have good English,' said Gagga. 'But they are very pleased you're here.'

Gagga's mother spoke to Shirley. Gagga said something back to her mother – chastising? – then turned to face Shirley.

'She says, Serbia is an odd choice for a holiday,' Gagga said.

'Yes,' Shirley said, 'I suppose it is. But I just wanted to, you know, be around different people, see some sights. This pie is really good by the way.'

Day 4

'Yes I'm still alive, Stuart. No I haven't found a hotel. No, a different friend. Yes I am making lots of new friends. It's that kind of place. What do you mean, I'm that kind of girl?'

Shirley imagined throwing the phone into the trees.

'Trying to find myself? Well, even if I was I'd have more luck than you, stabbing around with your tiny dick!'

She hurled the phone in the direction of the trees. Cheap, she thought, totally cheap, as she walked over and saw – thankfully – that the phone was still all in one piece. More than that, Stuart was still shouting down it. Standing five feet away, she couldn't make out the words, just the vibrations of a human voice, distorted slightly, like a foreign language. She stood there in the orchard, looking up at the apples, thinking how blissful ignorance was, until Stuart gave up and the noise suddenly stopped.

'Hey, yo! Hey yo yo you!'

Shirley spun round to see Milan posing by the hut in a pirate hat.

'You're insane!' she shouted.

He began running in circles, his tongue hanging out of his mouth.

This strip of paradise was Milan's kingdom. From the river to the road, twenty metres across, with a mud hut (self-built!) in the middle. Milan was a poet (self-taught!) and he lived here alone most weekends. He couldn't write in the flat in Novi Sad, with his parents in the next room. It was too much like masturbating. He was well known in Serbia although not rich (how could he be?). Awards were hung around the hut, where there was also a typewriter and a small stove.

Shirley picked up her phone and went back towards the hut. When she reached Milan he stopped running and said, 'Your husband!'

'Boyfriend,' she corrected.

'Ex?'

'No, but it feels that way. We haven't been being very... nice, to each other lately.'

'You build love, don't you. So carefully. And what are you left with? A beautiful ruin! Ha!'

Shirley laughed.

'Monuments to emptiness!' he continued. 'Here we are! Fifty dinars at the door! Roll up roll up!'

Milan stood with his hands on his hips, his blond hair white in the July sun. Ten years ago he had been in the army.

'Let's play badminton,' he said.

'Then will you take me to the train station?'

'Sure,' he said. 'Sure sure. You are still migrating south?'

'Yes,' she said. 'And this time I'm getting on the train.'

As she combed her hair she heard him marching up and down outside, singing something in Serbian. As she listened more closely she realised it was English, and a tune she knew. He was singing, 'Shir-ley I love you, I want to be your slave,' to the tune of 'Rule Britannia'. Then he slipped and swore.

Day 5

When her phone rang she didn't answer it. It was more embarrassment than strength of will, but it worked all the same. She ran outside the gallery and turned it off, quickly as she could.

An old man had followed her outside; now he stood against a pillar, staring. He was wearing an artist's smock – could he be? No it was too explicit – and his beard was straggly and old-dog grey. He pointed to her bracelet and spoke to her in Serbian.

'Sorry,' said Shirley, 'I'm English.'

'Oh,' he said, moving nearer. 'The bracelet is Serbian orthodox you know, like a rosary.'

'Yes. It was a present. I have Serbian friends.'

'None in Montenegro?'

'I arrived just this afternoon.'

'Nemanja,' he said, extending a hand. 'Cetinje's most celebrated painter.'

'Shirley. Which paintings are yours?'

'I will show you.'

He led her back into the gallery, along the cool, narrow corridors and up the stairs to a room where a single canvas stood against the wall.

'They are hanging it properly tomorrow,' he said.

'It's great,' said Shirley. She stared at the mass of oils – how angry the black and reds looked next to the pale blue wall.

'I was reading the other day that the two most popular adjectives in Serbian are 'catastrophic' and 'beautiful',' she said.

He offered her a cigarette.

'In here?'

'Yes,' he said, and she noticed how his beard carved a jut in the sparsely decorated room. 'We have our little freedoms.'

'I guess it's all about perspective.' She took a cigarette.

'So you came over here to feel lucky about your life?'

'No!' she said, outraged. Then she thought, *Did I?*

She stared at the painting, the unlit cigarette soft between her fingers.

She said, 'Yesterday I met a man who killed the cousin of his classmate in the war, without knowing. And where I work people are territorial about the milk they have in the fridge. You work out the difference – I'm fucking sick and tired of trying to work it all out.'

Then she turned on her heel. Halfway down the stairs he caught up with her.

'I am an artist,' he said. 'I do not have a head for calculations.'

She laughed.

'Milk, gods, mountains, whatever,' he said. 'They fight.'

'And what about love?'

'What about it! It is why they stop, if they stop. And when they

haven't got it, fear will do.'
    'I live my life perpetually afraid,' she said.
    'Ah, whatever works for you, sweetheart.'
    He said the 'heart' like he was hacking it up.
    Half an hour later she saved an old dog from being run over by a delivery van, literally stepped between the dog and the van with her hand up while the animal crossed. Nemanja applauded from the other side of the road, his smock shirt flapping in the breeze, his tired face smiling.
    'Everywhere you go you make a little history,' she said when she reached him, and he applauded again.

Day 6

'Yeah, I do feel better, thanks. It's not as though I came away for anything in particular.'
    She placed her hat on the stone lion's head. The lion was silently humiliated.
    'Just a bit of peace and quiet maybe.'
    The lion slept on.

Day 7

The man who drove the boat spoke no English. He and Shirley communicated by smiles, nods and shakes as they travelled out to the middle of the lake. Smiles at the honeyed dumplings and sliced goat's cheese, nods at the herons, shakes from him when she pointed out the distant hills of Albania. It was a cloudy day, with none of the heat and energy of the previous days, a different wash of colours and sounds.
    Shirley held her hat with one hand. With the other she dangled her phone over the edge of the boat, near the broken waves, wondering what dropping it in might achieve. Probably nothing. She put the phone back in her pocket. It was more complicated than that.
    They had accessed the lake via a small, turquoise tributary riddled with bulrushes and waterlilies. He had stopped the boat to pick her two flowers, a yellow and a white. He was a kind person, she could tell. But god knows what...

She knew that people didn't like talking about it but couldn't help themselves. And when you only had a few hours with someone there were certain things to be got past, things that could normally then be left behind and forgotten, eventually replaced. It was fortunate they shared no language.

At the centre of the lake she stood up, motioning wildly. He stopped the boat. She stretched her arms to the sky, where the clouds were raggedy as though they'd be painted too quickly with too little paint. She stood there, and he let her, expressionless, as she fixed the frame to just be lake and sky and mountains and clouds in view, like a picture. Like the drawings she used to do, with a sun in the top right corner of the page.

The Disfigurement

Patrick Belshaw

'Come and see me when you're ready, OK?'

As her voice sang out, I turned my head towards my bedroom door. I was just in time to catch sight of her as she skipped girlishly along the narrow hall to her room.

We had occupied our own rooms, never mind separate beds, for several years now. Not because our passion for one another had dried up. Far from it. We often made love with an intensity that our grown-up children would have thought improbable. Obscene, even.

It just seemed sensible, that's all. I like to sleep on my back, my arms and legs thrown wide apart, like a starfish, whereas she preferred to sleep on her side, knees curled up. The opposite, almost. More like a mollusc. I sometimes snore, too. You tend to, I think, when you sleep on your back. She, on the other hand, slept quiet and still as a mouse all night. Or so she liked to think.

'...And don't be too long!' she added.

'Yes, Mrs Ogmore-Pritchard!' I smiled as I unbuttoned the pyjama jacket I had just put on. 'Under Milk Wood' was a great favourite of ours. 'Just finishing my little tasks, my love – in order, if you please! Just closing the drawer marked pyjamas. Be with you in a minute.'

I always appreciated it when she declared her need like that. It told me she was ready. Spared me any embarrassment. Not that I was generally insensitive in these matters. I know I wasn't. Most of the time, anyway. But there were occasions, especially during the early years of our marriage, when I clumsily misread the signals. It happens to most men, I assume. So it was good to be given a clear, unequivocal message. It was good to know that she was as eager as I was.

However, on this occasion she had soared above mere eagerness. It was almost as if she knew.

'God, you're an animal, Jenny Wyndham!' I joked, when eventually I came up for air. 'A ravening animal!'

Coming out of my bedroom the next morning, I turned off the hall to go to the lavatory. I was still dazed from sleep as I pushed lightly against the door. It didn't immediately open.

'Sorry, Jen,' I called, veering off towards the kitchen to put the kettle on. 'Didn't realise you were up, love. Back in a few minutes with the tea.'

There was no answer. All was quiet. But by then I had almost moved out of earshot.

I liked the quiet. Liked those first few minutes of the day. Just me and the purring kettle. And the view across the valley.

When I went along the hall with the teas a short time later, the lavatory door was still closed. I pushed it with my foot. When it didn't give, I felt a slight twinge of unease. But I was not concerned. There was sure to be a simple explanation.

I put the cups down on the carpet and pushed against the door with my hands. It resisted the pressure. Now I felt a sudden flicker of concern. It wasn't locked! There was some give in the upper half of it. Not much. Just an inch or so. Very little lower down, though. And practically none at all at floor level. Something was blocking it on the inside. Something – and now I felt a stab of fear – was preventing the door from opening. My heart started thumping. It seemed to be beating inside my head. Banging against my ear drums. Sounding like waves hitting a shelf of shingle. I heard myself cry out – a strange cry, caught in the dryness of my throat.

I lunged at the door with my shoulder. It opened a couple of inches, perhaps. No more. Then it sprang back again. It was well and truly jammed. Now I really panicked.

I ran round to the lavatory window at the side of the cottage.

'Jen! Jen!' I called, again and again, as I banged on the window. 'Jen, can you hear me?' I was still in my pyjamas, and my bare feet, chilled by the concrete, were aching. 'Jen, are you all right?'

It was a silly question. I knew she wasn't.

'Answer me, Jen, if you can,' I croaked. But by now I was sure that she couldn't.

I banged repeatedly on the window, and between thumps I pressed my face close to the glass. Cupping my hands round my eyes, I tried to see inside. It was hopeless. The special glass distorted everything. In desperation, I made several attempts – several farcical attempts – to break the glass with my elbow, before giving up and running round to the garage for a hammer. Despite the cold, I was lathered in sweat.

On the way back, blinded by tears, I collided with the dustbin and fell heavily, tearing my pyjamas and grazing my knee. I cursed loudly as I got awkwardly to my feet, using the wall for support.

Surprisingly, I felt no hurt. By now, I could feel nothing. Nothing but fear. Fear and panic. And, already, a sickening sense of loss.

Almost before I smashed the glass, I think I knew it was all over. I knew, even before I saw her bottom-up body slumped grotesquely against the door, that I had lost her. From the dark, empty depths of my stomach, I just knew.

Even so, I was frantic to get to her. I tried pulling myself up and onto the window ledge, but it was too high. Desperate though I was, I just didn't have the strength. All I did was cut myself on a splinter of glass.

'Shit!' I cried, as I realised I would need the step-ladders. 'Oh, shit!'

Another trip to the garage. More delay.

I found myself running again. Breathing with difficulty this time. But I had to get to her quickly. Not to see if she was still alive: somehow I was sure she wasn't. But to do something about her naked bottom. That was my first priority. As soon as I got back with the ladders, and was able to step over the glass-strewn sill and down onto the lavatory seat, that was my first, my only, thought. I had to attend to that bare, unwiped bottom.

It was not so much that it offended my sensibilities, though to my surprise, it did; but rather that I knew it would have offended hers. Even in death (and she was dead, I was sure of that) I knew she had to be relieved of that indignity as quickly as possible. She would have hated anyone to see her in that condition. Oddly, me in particular.

Afterwards. Some time afterwards. Once I had recovered from the initial shock. I tried to work out what might have happened. It wasn't easy. My distress was still acute. The whole thing was to become a recurring nightmare for me.

One thing seemed certain: death had come without any warning. Even as I stepped down from the lavatory seat, trying to avoid the mess of faeces and broken glass, that much was obvious. Caught in the middle of her toilet, she must have pitched forwards suddenly, her feet touching the floor to act as the fulcrum for a turning movement.

But for the door, she would probably have turned a somersault. As it was, she had come to rest with her backside uppermost and her nightie in folds around her twisted trunk below.

Poor Jenny! I found it difficult to imagine her in a more undignified position. Her naked buttocks and thighs, rounded and enlarged by her unnatural posture, seemed to dominate the small space. I hated to see her like that. Body hideously deformed. Surrounded by mess. And that awful, unforgettable smell hanging in the air. Presiding, almost. She had always been so fastidious. Suddenly I felt sick, violently sick. Yet I didn't vomit. Nothing to bring up, I suppose.

As I wiped her bottom clean with a ball of toilet paper pulled from the roll, I guessed she had been dead for some time. Several hours, as far as I could judge. For one thing, her flesh felt cold and unnaturally firm. For another, her faeces had hardened and stuck to her body. To remove it, I had to wet the paper under the tap and soak her skin.

I still hadn't seen her face. Pushed up against the door, it was partially screened by her left forearm which looked as if it could have been thrown up for protection in a sort of reflex action. It was difficult to work it out, because her body parts were all out of position somehow. Nothing seemed to be where you might expect to find it. It was bizarre. I presumed it was the way her body had settled itself after cannoning into the door.

Two things now seemed important to me. Firstly, I had to try to straighten her out. Then I had to somehow drag her backwards towards the pedestal, so that I could get the lavatory door open and move her out into the hall. Only when I had done all this, when finally she lay across my outstretched body, her head cushioned in the crook of my arm – only at that point could I bring myself to look at her face.

'Jen,' I heard myself croaking. 'Oh, Jenny, my love, where are you?'

I was still panting from my exertions, and a mixture of sweat and tears dripped from my chin onto her long, white neck.

'Where have you gone?' She was scarcely recognisable to me. I heard the despair rising in my voice. 'Please, Jen, where have you gone?'

Listening to myself going on like that, I felt embarrassed. Ashamed, almost. But try as I did – and I did try desperately hard – I could find little resemblance between the lifeless body I held in my arms and the woman I had embraced so passionately a few hours earlier. In fact, and it broke me, filled me with shame, to admit it, I found her corpse repellent.

It wasn't so much the physical disfigurement. I had been confronted with far worse in my life. No, it was something else. Something I couldn't describe adequately – until the phrase, 'the disfigurement which is death itself', came into my mind. From where? CS Lewis, perhaps..? Somebody like that. Anyway, it rang a bell. Nothing in life quite matched, quite prepared you for, that hideous disfigurement. Nothing could help you deal with the cold, flat ugliness of death.

'I can leave that with you, then..?'

I could hear someone saying this. The voice was distant, detached, dispassionate. Not mine, surely? No, it couldn't be mine. Yet I had heard it before. And wasn't that my hand holding the phone..?

No, impossible! A crossed line, then? Of course! This was some fellow, sounding very matter-of-fact, very business-like, who appeared to be ringing the Council. The refuse collection department, from what I could gather. Arranging to have something taken away. Some unwanted domestic item, by the sound of it.

'Good... oh, that's kind... I'm sorry to inconvenience you... I'll wait in then, shall I?... till you call..? Okay. Goodbye.'

It was my hand that put the phone down. A hand like mine, anyway. A hand with a liver spot just below the middle knuckle.

Ah, well! I made my way along the hall to the bathroom. For what purpose, I don't think I could have told you. To pee, presumably.

And suddenly, there she was. In my path. Her body. Laid out on the carpet. Blocking my way.

The sight of her did not disturb me. How strange that was! In fact, I simply stepped round her. Avoiding her. As one might, for the moment, avoid an item that would need tidying away later.

Redemption

David Lambert

Father Louis J. McKinlon of Our Lady of the Martyrs Chapel, squat in his soiled cassock still untied at the waist, rifled the pages in desperate search of consolation. Ecclesiastes, Mark. Or perhaps Luke. Trembling fingers still with her scent on them, flipped the gilt-edges, light as tracing paper, flimsy as reputation. Pursed lips mouthed the well-worn phrases... *foul lusts... Thou shalt not covet... Vengeance is mine.* Nothing! The winged armchair creaked under his sudden weight.

Through shuttered jalousie windows, their slats lowered like furtive eyes on the mid-morning sun, Father McKinlon gazed down the hillside over the rusty roofs of scattered shacks, to the broad swathe of beach below. The surf was rolling in, as it had done since he was a boy, spreading high over the sand like a dirty lace ruff. Further off, the cliffs of Canaan rose up, their rocky frowns smoothed by distance. In the silence, the neighbour's goat, tethered below the window, cropped the long grass, its extended rope chaffing against the raised concrete pillars.

'Chloe... Chloe', moaned the priest. He heard the chapel bell ringing out down the hillside. Eleven o'clock. Brother Francis calling the faithful to their knees. He imagined the gaggle of penitents waiting outside the creaking oak confessional. *Forgive me Father for I have sinned.* Today they would go without absolution.

It was not the first time the housekeeper had sent her daughter in her stead. Eugenia had taken the bus to the bank over in Montegordo, and promised she'd be back by evening to prepare supper. Whenever Eugenia took to her bed with a 'sugar high', Chloe would skip morning school. She'd sweep the presbytery floors and make his big iron-frame bed. Then she'd prepare the midday meal for when he returned from chapel. He'd find stewed chicken and pigeon peas laid out on the dining room table, wrapped in tin foil under gauze fly covers, everything just as her mother did, even the lace cover placed on the water jug, and the drinking glass turned upside down.

The chapel bell stopped tolling. The wall clock's regular beat grew intolerable. Father McKinlon closed the Bible, stood up, and steadied himself against the writing desk. Brother Francis would soon be up to find out what was wrong. His eyes travelled around the parlour, its hard armchairs and nests of tables, the motes of dust dancing in the rays of light coming through the jalousies, and back to the writing desk where he'd written so many sermons. Through the doorway, the dining room table stood abandoned, half laid.

He tied the loose rope of his cassock. As he made his way over the dark floorboards, he heard them creak. Opening the door to the veranda, he stepped into blinding light.

As he made his way down the beaten earth path he could hear their cries. Mid-morning break, like the raucous chatter of monkeys coming through the big leaved foliage. He could make out laughter, wild and free, outraged shrieks, one rising high above the others: *No! No! Ah say lemme beee!* Halfway down the hill the playground came into view. Small dark bodies in khaki and blue dodged and ducked. The school buildings had changed little since he'd attended it over forty years ago, the rusting tin roof and the streaked distemper unpainted since the rainy season. The playground was now cemented over, a high wire fence running around its perimeter. Teenage boys and girls lolled against it, flirting. He could not see her among them. She would hardly have gone back to school. What if she had run straight home? He held his breath and became aware of the blood pumping in his ears. When did a child become a woman?

At the foot of the hill by the big immortelle tree was the Ragoobar shack. In his day, it had been old Mrs Ragoobar, the mother, in her sari and wrist bangles, handing out brown paper twists of channa for sweaty coins. Now it was Gupta, who'd been at school with him, who waited for recess and going-home time by the roadside. Had Gupta seen Chloe fleeing down the path, barefoot, her uniform torn and dishevelled? Gupta would point her finger and screech out his foul deed for the whole school to hear. As he drew level, he saw no one at the serving hatch, but a rustling was coming from within; she must have bent down to get something. Breaking out in a cold sweat, the priest hastened his pace and sneaked by.

To get to the Canaan cliffs, without meeting anyone, he'd have to walk along the pitch road for a stretch before he could swing inland onto higher ground. To his right, blades of sugar cane rustled, and from somewhere inside the field a labourer was hacking with a machete. White- tails swooped over the high tops of the crop. There was little traffic at this hour; a half empty taxi slowed and pipped him. He waved it on without turning. A Mercedes van sped by on its way to the big new hotel on Canaan Heights.

His heart was pounding unnaturally. The girl lived in the housing settlement just along the main road past the canefield where the village began. If she had run home, which he now felt sure she must have, her brother Elvin would have seen the state she was in, and be coming along the road up to the presbytery with his machete. He was a good for nothing who brawled outside the rum shop on Friday nights. He sometimes worked nights on the fishing boats, but usually spent all day sprawling in a hammock under the house. Father McKinlon turned off the hot pitch road into a dirt trace which would take him up into the bush. Coming along the trace, he immediately saw two of his parishioners, Mammie James and her simple daughter Agnes. The women were negotiating the ruts in their best shoes, hitching up satin skirts. He could not turn back; he drew a breath and continued towards them. When Mammie James looked up from under the gauze of her hat, her old eyes popped with incomprehension.

'Beh! Father? Wha'ya doin' here?' Even Agnes looked perplexed.

'Good day, ladies,' he tried to steady his voice. Sweat was welling from his armpits and running down the inside of his cassock. He was still unsure what he could say. 'Mammie James, Miss Agnes'.

'Yuh ent suppos' tuh be takin' confession, Father?' said the older woman.

'I have a parishioner to see... but Brother Francis is at the chapel. Tell him to proceed without me.' He attempted a smile to reassure her, but this only seemed to increase her bewilderment. She saw his loathsomeness, read abomination on his features. He hurried on, and felt saucer eyes staring after him.

Further along, the rutted trace narrowed to a beaten earth track used by the village boys to take the goats to higher pasture. He tugged at his collar. He felt it resist, then pop as the button went spinning off into the bush. Sobbing out loud, he flung the starched white loop into a gully of nettles and stumbled on, blinded by tears and self-loathing. That skinny little girl child! She was transformed since Eugenia used to bring her up to the house. Now, when Chloe replaced the mother he tried to be out, or else he stayed in the parlour and drew the inadequate calico curtain across the connecting doorway to the kitchen, still acutely aware of her on the other side, the timid clang of cooking pots, the tread of her damson soles on the floorboards. He was wicked, he'd seen the revulsion in Mammie James' eyes. *Unlawful lust! Abomination! Hypocrite!* And there was Elvin with his machete. He wanted it only to end. He could smell the sea now, taste its briny sting upon his tongue. A little further on he could hear the dull battering of the waves against the cliff face at Canaan. The sea roared its wrath, sending up hallelujahs of white spume which dropped back onto the rocks below. The tonnage of water would pulverise odious flesh, grind bones like grist between millstones, removing all trace from this world.

He emerged from the bush onto a deserted grassy area at the cliff top where coconut palms with tattered fronds swayed in the sea blast. The ground was strewn with coconuts, some green and freshly fallen, others brown and dented. Approaching the cliff through the slender trunks, he was suddenly aware of a woman standing on the edge. Her pale hair was plastered to her head, her wet dress flapping against her legs. He felt intense irritation; he was not alone, what was she doing here? He saw her calf muscles tighten as she braced herself against the wind. She took a half step towards the edge, tensing herself, craning her neck to look onto the rocks below. At any moment a wall of sea spray would rise up and when it fell she would no longer be there.

'Hey!' he shouted. But his voice was carried off in the wind. He strode forwards, and stopped some ten yards off. 'Excuse!' When she turned, it was not at his call but the louder flap of his cassock skirts in the wind. Red rimmed eyes, a thin contorted face – was it anger, or the shock of seeing him so close behind her? He held out his hand while she stood glaring at him. 'Come away from the edge. Please...'

He saw her glance back at the cliff edge. All she had to do was step off it. If she relaxed her calf muscles for a second, a squall of wind would snatch her over. He felt he'd seen this white woman before somewhere. Yes, in town earlier in the week, by the craft market. She'd been with a large fair man, who was shouting at her in German or Dutch. He'd shoved his ugly bearded face right up to hers. Yes, it was her, that look of terror in the eyes.

He beckoned with his outstretched hand. Come, come. He saw her bend at the knees. Was she kneeling to pray? Instead, she picked up a green coconut lying beside her and, standing up, lobbed it over the edge. Then she backed away from the cliff and turning, came towards him, her face waxen, her lips twisted. They said nothing as she followed his still offered hand away from the sea blast into the quiet of the sea grape trees. There was a rotting wooden bench under one of them. He sat down cautiously and thought she might do the same, but she stood her ground, her back half turned to him, her arms folded. He noticed she was trembling.

'I'm sorry...' he said.

She turned to look at him now, rage and suspicion on her small pinched features. Perhaps she didn't understand English. She tightened her arms across her chest and he noticed blue and yellow smudges on the white undersides of her arms. 'What are you... a Father?' she spoke with an accent. 'Where is your..?' she pointed with her lips.

He put his hand to his neck, and felt only exposed collarbones. 'I'm Father McKinlon,' was all he could think to say.

'How did you know I am up here?' she spat out.

'I didn't.' He could hardly tell her why he was there. 'I was taking a walk.' The woman heard this with what seemed deep mistrust. She was about forty, plain with small grey eyes made red and puffy. Her hair, the colour of dirty sand, was stiff and stringy with salt. 'Are you staying at the hotel?' he asked. She glared at him but did not answer. 'I believe I saw you, the other day, in town, at the craft fair.' Still she said nothing, but he noticed her pupils constrict slightly. 'You were with your husband...?'

'What you know about my husband?' she said in alarm.

'Nothing. Just... he wasn't being very nice to you'.

'You have been following me, yes! You followed me up here! This is not your business! What you know about me?' she took a step backwards, as if she might run. He held up his hands.

'Calm yourself. I know nothing about you. Except that you are suffering.' The woman continued to hold him in her pale stare as if trying to make sense of him, a black priest, his dog collar ripped, appearing to her on the deserted cliffs. 'I had to stop you', he said.

She took a step back towards the bench, her face mobile; she might burst into sobs or fall at his feet. Tears welled at her small, almost colourless eyes and she breathed heavily. Slowly she lifted and held out her bare arms, elbows together, so that the unsightly marks were exposed. 'I can't...' she started, then shook her head. 'Look what he does to me!' Father McKinlon found it hard to look at the naked white arms held up to him like an accusation. 'I thought, yes, it's better that I end it...'

'It is a sin, my child,' he heard himself saying.

'Who will know..? The sea it carries everything away, far away. I heard you have sharks here, yes? So they can never find the body... No one will ever know!'

'God sees everything. Sooner or later we all have to answer to the Almighty.' It was a response Father McKinlon had given to other desperate souls. But sitting on the rotting bench under the sea grape tree on Canaan Heights with this white tourist and her bruised arms, he was for the first time convinced of its truth. The woman sat down slowly on the edge of the worm-eaten bench, her hands clasped between her knees. She stared at the ground.

'Father,' she said eventually. 'Can you forgive me... for my action... give me... what is it?'

'Absolution? You haven't yet committed any sin, my child'.

She looked at him as if a burden had lifted, her eyes widened and her lips spread slightly to reveal a sharp incisor. 'No,' she said. 'You are right. You saved me.'

A great white tower of spume rose up at the cliff face, its fine spray reached them on the bench, sharp and salty. Silver clouds billowed out above the dark blue expanse of sea and paler sky. Along the coast, in the village, they would be going up to the presbytery to look for him, machetes in their hands. If not now, then as soon as Eugenia got back from town and found her daughter withdrawn and listless, her school uniform torn. *But who it is did this to yuh, chile? Which piece o' nastiness? Who it was? Tell me nuh, gyal!* She would beat it out of her. *It de Pries', Ma! Father McKinlon!* Mammie James would tell them she'd met him on the path up to Canaan. He'd be dragged back to public humiliation, unfrocked, thrown in jail... He gave a nervous glance over his shoulder into the dense bush.

Seeing this, the woman started. 'Who is there..? You have come with someone!' she stood up, scrutinizing the bush. 'You *have* followed me!'

He found it odd she should so care what others might think of her. He tried to calm her, to tell her he was alone, that he hadn't known she'd be there. Desperate to convince her, he even told her God had sent him, and part of him wondered if indeed he had, and that it might cost him his reputation – his life – to save this tourist woman. She was still casting anxious looks at the bush.

'It's me they'll be coming after.' He saw her eyes flick to his hands which were gripping his knees through the black cloth of his cassock in an effort to stop them shaking.

'W-what is wrong with you?' she asked. 'And where is your collar… Your button, it's missing.'

'I've committed a sin, a terrible sin'. He felt better once he'd said it. He noticed an immediate shift in her, more open, more sympathetic. She even sat back down and leaned forward slightly to hear what he might say. 'You see… I came up here for the same reason you did'. He looked towards the cliff, and felt her small eyes staring at him in utter disbelief, stunned into silence. She was no doubt grappling with the realisation that, however unlikely it seemed, they were in the same boat, her saviour himself in need of rescue. But he knew their boats were entirely different; she was the abused.

After a long time, she said softly, 'You saved me. Whatever you have done, you have done good now, so it is… cancelled, yes?'

Oh, if only it were so! He was only relieved she didn't enquire about the nature of his sin. Europeans had tact; perhaps it was simply reserve. Or indifference. She probably imagined a petty misdemeanour, something a trembling middle-aged priest on a small island might be capable of, drinking the communion wine or putting his hand in the collection box. If she knew the reality, she would not be leaning towards him so sympathetically in this isolated spot.

'Where is your husband?' he asked after some time. The mention of him made her start. Anguish passed across her features, as if she had momentarily forgotten. 'Is he at the hotel?'

She looked at him, fearful, and said in half a voice. 'Yes. That's right.' She leaned back on the bench and squinted at the glittering sea. 'I don't want to die… you're right, that would be a terrible mistake, a sin like you say. I want to start to live. Thank you.'

In the late afternoon, Father McKinlon made his way back along the coast. In preventing Ilse, the white tourist, from taking her life, he felt he could not now do so himself. If they wanted him, they would come and get him in their own time. He'd face the consequences of his actions.

The shadows were lengthening as he walked around the broad sweep of the bay and watched the surf reach its foamy fingers up the beach. He turned to see in the distance the dark frowning cliff face.

Passing the school, he noticed the gates already shut and padlocked, the premises deserted. Gupta Ragoobar was still in her shack. She paused as she was closing the serving hatch and gave him a sleepy 'A'right?' Up at the presbytery, the neighbour's goat had cut a circular swathe of grass around its tether. He found a note wedged in the veranda door from Brother Francis. His young assistant assumed he'd gone to read the last rites to old man Moses; he'd expect him at six for chapel. Father McKinlon pushed the door open.

He sat in the hard armchair and waited. A solitary fly buzzed a crooked flight path across the room and bumped into the parchment lamp shade on the writing desk. The Bible was still where he had left it, closed and silent. As evening drew on, the pattern cast by the sun through the jalousies shifted round the walls before finally fading. Still he heard no heavy footsteps on the veranda, no shouts, no fists banging at the door. Everything seemed normal.

At six o'clock, the chapel bell started to toll out over the hillside. He rose wearily from his chair. After standing in the middle of the room some minutes, he cleared the half laid dining room table. The lettuce in the Pyrex bowl had gone brown in the heat and started to putrify; he tipped the slimy mess into the kitchen bin. Then he washed his hands at the sink and dried them on some kitchen roll. He crossed to his bedroom and took from the top drawer of the dresser a fresh dog collar which he placed under his cassock and carefully buttoned down. Then he went out the veranda door down to the chapel.

A small congregation of a dozen or so older women were sitting in the pews when he arrived. He stood at the lectern reading the Psalms, and each time he lifted his eyes to the double doors at the back of the chapel, he was surprised not to see strange men slipping in. He got through the simple service somehow and took confession from three of those attending, in the box at the back of the church, no more than a lopsided wardrobe. Their petty sins irritated him. He heard them out, granting each a hastily muttered penance. He had told Brother Francis he could leave early, and was locking up the vestry when he heard someone in the chapel, the thud of a heel resounding against a wooden pew. So, it was here they'd come for him! He waited but could hear nothing more than the bullfrogs whistling in the ravine. As he went to the vestry door he saw her. She was sitting in the twilight in the last row of pews.

'Father', she said as he approached her. 'I had to see you before I go.'

He sat down in the pew in front of her and turned back. Her eyes were made up and her mouth reddened with lipstick. He noticed she'd covered her arms in long sleeves and had a small leather handbag with her. 'Your holiday is over so soon? I hope you'll seek help, tell someone about your predicament, perhaps when you get back to your country.'

'I'm not going back to Norway. I'm leaving my husband.' She said it with defiance, as if to see his reaction, as a small child might threaten to leave home. But she was clearly terrified. He looked at her and nodded slowly. This was none of his business, he had enough on his plate. 'Where will you go?'

She took a small breath, as if slightly thrown by his calm acceptance, prepared to protest and argue. She said, 'There's a flight to Caracas tonight. I have money, I have a credit card, he'll never find me…'

As she spoke he became aware of the faint smell of petrol; a car engine was throbbing on the hill outside the chapel. 'I have a taxi waiting. Before I go, Father, I want you to give me your blessing.'

Eugenia had come in and made supper and left it under tin foil and fly gauze on the dining table. Unless it was the daughter? He inspected the kitchen. No, that was precisely the way Eugenia folded the dishcloth in four and placed it on top of the cooker to dry in the heat from the oven pilot. Her apron was hanging as usual behind the door, slightly damp from her habit of drying her hands across her belly. The girl had not told, then. Might things really return to normal, was this a reprieve? Was he being granted a second chance? Perhaps Ilse was right in saving her life he'd redeemed himself in the eyes of the Almighty, who really did see everything! He would make it up to Chloe, beg her forgiveness, provide a scholarship for her education! Father McKinlon got down on his knees right there in the presbytery parlour and offered up thanks, his hands clasped so tight his knuckles showed yellow.

The next morning, he was at his writing desk when Eugenia came up. He watched her eyes and listened closely to her voice, but could discern nothing altered, no attitude, no resentment. He heaved a sigh and silently offered more thanks to God. Eugenia chatted on, all about the long lines in the bank, the heat and then the bus breaking down on the journey home. She even said she hoped Chloe looked after him good.

He was opening the jalousie slats when he noticed an ambulance, as small as a toy, parked down on the road by the beach. A police car was beside it and a small dark crowd had gathered. Young boys were running excitedly from the road and into the surf, beach dogs yapping at their heels. A couple of policemen were unrolling a tape to cordon off the area. Not another fisherman drowned? There had been no storms.

He heard the regular swish of Eugenia's broom behind him. She stopped and looked over the priest's shoulder. 'Looks like something happened', he said.

'Yuh ent hear, Father? Is a body they find. A white tourist.'

Father McKinlon turned to her. He didn't know what to think. 'Man or woman?' he asked.

'White is all I does know,' said Eugenia primly. 'Police, the radio people all down there. I pass 'em on my way up. There goin' to be a whole set o' fuss.'

Later that morning, once Eugenia had cooked and laid out his midday meal and left until the evening, he tried to settle to opening his mail with the engraved paper knife the Diocese had presented him; it was shaped like the Sword of Truth. There was a request to address a local school on the Christian notion of discipleship, and an invitation from an ecumenical gathering to talk on the sanctity of life. He stood up from his writing desk and looked out on the beach with mounting anxiety. It was entirely cordoned off now, just some policemen taking measurements and journalists making a broadcast. At three o'clock he turned on the radio with a feeling of dread. The newscast reported the body of a Norwegian tourist carried down the coast by prevailing currents and washed up in Pirates' Bay. Olaf Nielsen had been a guest at Canaan Heights Hotel. According to the island coroner, injuries to the head of the victim suggest cause of death as a blow to the head by a blunt instrument. The police are anxious to know the whereabouts of the deceased's wife, Mrs Ilse Nielsen, also missing, before they can rule out a double tragedy.

An unopened letter still in his hand, Father McKinlon turned and stumbled to his desk where he sat down heavily. He closed his eyes and saw only the bright jalousie slats imprinted like neon. Between intermittent flashes, he saw her bracing herself on the cliff top after the act, stretching her neck for a final glimpse to the rocks below, bending down to pick up the incriminating coconut and tossing it into the sea. He recalled her intense suspicion of him – how much had he seen? She had planned it all, reckoning even on the presence of sharks to devour the body. And then come to him to get his blessing! And he had given it, oh how he had given it! Indebted to this stranger who had held out to him his only chance of redemption, he had knelt down with her on the stone chapel floor and thanked God for deliverance of them both.

Towards nightfall, when Eugenia came back to prepare the priest's supper, she wondered that he was not at chapel but still in his parlour, slumped oddly in a circle of lamplight over his reading. The clock on the wall tocked the passing seconds. And still he remained there motionless, the first moths knocking themselves against the parchment lampshade.

'Father,' she started. No reply. She cleared her throat and stepped cautiously on a dark floorboard which she knew creaked. No response. 'I goin' an' start to cook… It have some kingfish in the fridge.'

His silence was almost unbearable. Is somet'ing she done, or ent done? An' why he lef' the jalousies open so, an' night fallin'? Finding her purpose, the housekeeper walked over to the window, more confident now, but her eyes never left the figure slumped over the desk. She noticed the shiny brown hand hanging heavily by his side, and that the sandaled foot was turned in at an odd angle. It was almost as if these minor incongruities were more alarming to her than the sight of the substance, brown as molasses, which spread out from the priest's chest and spilled over the gilt edging of the book to gather in a small lake at the scalloped edge of the desk, retained only by surface tension.

Under the presbytery jalousies, the goat raised its head, startled by the housekeeper's cry which rent the darkening night. In momentary trepidation, it blinked yellow glass-eyes, before it returned to cropping the long sweet grass.

Revelations of Divine Love

Annie Kirby

I

The girl with red hair is standing on a box, between Tesco Metro and the covered market, surrounded by huddles of soberly dressed men and women pressing tracts into the hands of passers-by. Sunshine unfurls through the sycamore leaves, suffusing her face with stippled light.

'I saw the bloodless face of Christ,' she says. 'He was vivid, so beautiful that I reached up to touch his skin, to trace the frown lines on his forehead, but my fingers pricked the crown of thorns and blood ran down his face, then, and onto my hands.'

Vivid. Hearing that word from her lips again, it grips my insides, wrings them out. I hadn't know what vivid truly meant until I knew her. She looks exactly the same as the last time I saw her, that day fifteen years ago on Bryn Celyn when she turned her head and smiled goodbye, before the ferns closed around her like claws and she disappeared into the valley. Pinafore, thick tights, plain shoes. Except that today she's wearing a black headscarf that can't disguise the auburn hair flickering across her temples. Last time I saw her, her hair was loose and wet, twisting down her back, studded with droplets of river water that flashed in the sun.

Her accent is different; the Geordie lilt has ebbed away over the years. But her voice still makes the blood pump through my heart in tides.

'Mam,' says Carly, tugging at my elbow, 'Mam, can we go now?'

I twist my arm out of her grip and there's a faint tinkling sound as the shopping bags scatter across the pavement. It's the teapot that's broken, the one from Whittard's with the gerbera on the side.

'Mam?'

Carly, unsure of whether to follow me or pick up the shopping, hesitates and then I'm free of her, striding across the road, shoving my way through the gaggle of God-botherers.

'I was thirty and one half years old,' the girl with red hair is saying, 'when a terrible bodily sickness fell upon me.'

Thirty is the age she ought to be, the same as me, but she still looks fifteen, the age she was when she bathed in the pool where my brother drowned, her hair mushrooming through the water like blood; the day I traced the pattern of silvery scars on her belly with my thumb and thought they looked like cobwebs in the rain.

She notices the commotion, breaks off in mid-sentence. Silence rushes in like river water to fill up the space left by her voice. Now that I'm up close, I can see that her eyes are paler than I remember, more grey than green. I take a breath, meaning to say her name, but I'm seized by a momentary blankness and what hovers on my lips is 'vivid', a word that is almost as beautiful as she. Then her name, the name that has possessed my dreams for fifteen years, uncurls onto my tongue.

'Juliana,' I say, and my voice sounds like glass breaking, 'Juliana.'

She blinks at me. 'Do I know you?'

'Juliana, don't you recognise me? I'm Teleri.'

There's movement to the side of me, stirring through the crowd.

'Juliana,' I say, again.

'My name's not Juliana. I don't know anyone called that.'

And then it hits me, why she hasn't aged. Why she's still fifteen. How could I have been so stupid?

'Grace?' I say. 'Grace Donnelly?'

She relaxes a little, her shoulders slanting downwards.

'Yes,' she says. 'I'm Grace.'

'I knew your sister,' I say, tears stinging my eyes.

Grace's face clouds over. 'I don't have a sister.'

'Juliana? Maggie? Maggie Donnelly?' I hear the desperation in my voice, can't control it.

Grace is staring around now, hoping for someone to come and rescue her from this madwoman. And someone does. He lays a hand across my forearm.

'Leave her alone, girl,' he says.

He hasn't changed, except his hair is grey now. His voice is still mild, charming even, and the vanilla fragrance of his cigar coils into the sycamore leaves in pale wisps. I think of Juliana, the wounds etched onto her body, and the web of silvery scars on her belly and abdomen. I look at Grace, who is so like her. I didn't know what those silvery scars were, not then, when I was fifteen.

Grace smiles. A sweet, unfocused smile that carries her away from her father and the madwoman in the market square. I've seen that smile before and it turns my body to mist. I don't even feel the pavement as it rushes up to meet me. Someone is holding my hair, rubbing my back. It's Carly, my sweet, lovely Carly.

'Mam,' she says. 'Mam. Are you okay?'

I uncurl slowly, like an old woman. Grace and her father have gone, melted into the crowd, and Juliana is just a ghost again.

II

I set off early, walking along the old Farrow Road to the edge of town, then following the bank of the Gwri-fawr, pushing through river mist and fern fronds. Most days, rain wrapped itself around the valley like a veil. It drew us together, but it kept us apart from the other towns scattered between the mountains. It didn't matter how far up Bryn Celyn you climbed, the thick mist of cloud meant you couldn't see beyond the twin rivers twisting side by side at one edge, or the ghost colliery and the corrugated roof of the Honda factory on the other. Once in a while the sun unfurled behind the clouds, filling them up with pale light instead of rain, and the sky would turn to silver, but most of the time Cwmcelyn was grey sky, grey houses, grey people, grey rain.

But the sun was shining on the day it started, which is why I was on the edge of the mountain at half past six in the morning.

The last time the sun had been shining had been a Sunday in March and it was the day Dyl died. Well, maybe he died the day before, nobody knows for definite, but in the morning when they came to tell us, the sun was leaking around the edges of my curtains and I was pressing my face into the cool side of the pillow. They found him floating in the pool where the Gwri-fach and Gwri-fawr rivers come together, face down with his jacket ballooning up over the surface of the water. It was kids that found him, little ones from the junior school who'd gone up to see if their newspaper and nail-varnish boats would survive the drop from the edge of the waterfall.

The Courier said Dyl's blood alcohol level was three times the legal limit but I don't know why they thought that was important 'cause he wasn't driving anywhere, didn't even own a car though he worked in the Honda factory putting bits of engines together. He just walked by himself into the valley after a night drinking in the Tafarn Glendower and jumped into the river.

I couldn't get the image of Dyl's swollen jacket out of my mind. It lingered for months. And when I'd woken up that morning to a halo of sunlight I'd felt sick with grief. I dozed a bit and dreamt of when we were little and Dad was spinning Dyl around by the shoulders of his snow-washed jacket, all the while Mam laughing and screaming at them to stop. Then that dream slipped into another one, Dyl's jacket, the snow-washed one I mean, turning in the waterfall pool, with him all green and drowned underneath. I ran into the bathroom and puked in the toilet, then sat in the kitchen making snail trails in the butter with the knife, and decided to go up there so I could look at the pool without Dyl's body floating in it and see if I felt any better.

So there I was. Between the mountain and the river, water rushing over rocks and the sun filtering down through the trees in layers. The two rivers flow in tandem for miles, edging closer to one another as they twist down the slopes of the Bryn-y-Llys and through the valley along the base of Bryn Celyn. An hour's walk into the valley the Gwri-fach veers off at an angle, scurries across a rocky outcrop and drops into the rumbling Gwri-fawr below, so that there's a waterfall and a deep, clear pool before the Gwri-fawr gathers itself together and continues alone down to the ocean. Before Dyl died, we used to swim up there, lads jumping off the waterfall in their keks, girls paddling in the shallows. I'd somehow made the waterfall further away in my mind than it really was, and the mingling of the different beats of the rivers, one low and breathy, the other flitting across pebbles, took me by surprise.

To get to the pool itself you either had to jump off the waterfall, or wade across and slide down a steep slope on your arse, hacking through a mass of ferns and bramble. You'd think that with all the rain, the rivers would be bursting at their seams, but what we got was mostly drizzle that barely licked the rivers' thirst. So the Gwri-fach was shallow and I hardly even got my trainers wet. I stood at the top of the slope for a bit, thinking I should turn around and go home, and then my ankle turned on a rock and I crashed through the ferns, feeling them slither and rip as I tumbled, landing on my knees in the dirt at the edge of the pool. I had mud on my jeans and scratches on my hands. I stood up painfully, feeling the bruises already beginning to blossom on my knees.

There was a body in the pool, face down, clouds of black fabric and red hair floating on the surface.

All the breath emptied out of me and I was weightless, floating. I bent over and puked on my trainers. It went on for ages, even though it was only a cup of tea with two sugars. I wiped a string of sick from the side of my mouth, getting it in my hair. I held my breath and looked back at the body. The blanket of red hair streamed across the surface like seaweed. Then the body stood up, water falling away in billows, and I screamed. I couldn't help it. She saw me and froze, one hand up against the side of her head, the other held out in front of her like she was about to put a key in a lock.

'I wasn't spying on you,' I said.

It was an idiot thing to say, but I couldn't think of anything else. The water in the pool rippled around her, nudging against the floating fan-shape of her dress. The contrast between the shifting water and the motionless girl made me dizzy, or maybe it was the fall, and I sat down hard in the mud.

It was the Donnelly girl. Maggie, Marjorie, I couldn't remember. She was a freak, the new girl nobody liked. She wore a long, black, high-necked dress and fingerless gloves, even in summer. On her first day at school, according to Linda who was in her maths class, she'd told everyone her name was Julian and she'd been granted three gifts from God. After a few days of people laughing at her and calling her a freakoid she stopped talking altogether, took to creeping along the corridors with her arms bent up around her head like someone was about to punch her.

I saw her once, in the girls' toilets when I was showing Linda the frilly knickers I'd liberated from Marks and Sparks in the city. The new girl's nostrils were wild and trembly, the way my cat Lulu got when a dog barked on the telly. I felt sorry for her because she was so strange and timid and friendless, but not bad enough to invite her to sit with us at lunchtimes or anything. Then Dyl died and I didn't give her another thought.

She didn't look all hunched over and scared now. She looked almost, you know, queenly. Her hair fell over her shoulders in thick, sodden tresses, water running off in points. She lowered her arms, pulled her elbows in tight to her waist.

'Did you fall?'

I shook my head, even though I had. The scratches on my hands were starting to sting. She waded towards me, her dress pressed into her body by the weight of the water.

'Did you fall?' she said, again.

'No,' I tried to answer, but my throat felt all crumpled and it came out more like a burp than a word. I burst into tears, big hitching gulps, just as she stepped onto the bank.

Her feet were bare, pale and tiny, mother-of-pearl sinking into dark mud. She disappeared, wet dress swishing, and came back with a hanky. She put her arm around me. It was embarrassing, bawling like a baby in front of the school freak, but I couldn't stop myself. I wanted to push her arm off me, but it seemed rude, since she'd just lent me her hanky. When I finally pulled myself together, she rinsed the hanky out in the pool and dabbed at the grazes on my hands and arms. Her hands were small and pretty, like her feet. She held them oddly, curled up a bit, and I caught a glimpse of a rust-red scar on her palm. She didn't have any freckles. I'd thought all people with red hair had freckles. When she'd finished cleaning up my scratches she scrubbed away at the puke on my trainers, and I sat there like a baby, letting her. She buried the filthy hanky in the mud, poking it down deep with her finger.

The pool was peaceful, all the different water sounds toning in so well with each other it was like Mozart or someone had arranged it. My face was all stretched and tight from crying. I knew I ought to say thank you, but I couldn't quite bring myself to do it.

'Do you want a drink of water?'

She had a pretty, sing-songy accent. I nodded and she passed me a flask. I took a swallow of the tepid, leady tasting water. Her eyes were green, the same colour as the feathered edges of ferns.

'My brother drowned in this pool,' I said, by way of explaining my hysterics.

'I know. You're Teleri Phillips. You're in my year at school. You're going out with Liam Thomas.'

Well, that made me feel bad, 'cause she knew my name and I wasn't sure about hers. And a little bit freaked out, too, that she knew so much about me.

'What's your name again?' I said.

'Julian.'

I wasn't sure how to respond to that. 'I thought it was Margaret.'

'No, it's Julian.'

She leant towards me, put her hand in my hair and I flinched.

'Money-spider,' she said, parting my highlights with her fingers and gently drawing the spider out. She held it up to the light where it swayed on its own thread, before swinging away into the trees.

'Thanks.'

'Your hair smells nice,' she said.

'It's just shampoo. Coconut. From the Co-op.'

'I've never used shampoo from a shop,' she said, pulling her knees into her chest, wrapping her black dress around her shins.

'What do you wash your hair with, then?'

'Eggs.'

'Doesn't it get all scrambled?'

She laughed, then. It sounded like the rush of the waterfall; deep, open and free. It shocked me, to hear it, 'cause it didn't seem quite right, what with her in that black dress looking nearly like a nun, that she should laugh like that.

'You have to use cold water, pet,' she said.

Her hair was drying in the sun. It was long, trailing down her back in heaps. It wasn't ginger but auburn with a rhubarby pink tinge that fizzed in the light. That fizzing, it made me think that if you put her hair in your mouth it would be like having sherbet or Space Dust on your tongue. She took a bunch of it in her hand, held it out to me. It was soft and springy. I sniffed it. It didn't smell of eggs, but of river water and something else, sharp and tangy.

'Vinegar,' she said, 'to make it shine.'

She started to plait her damp hair, slowly, expertly, criss-crossing the strands and pulling them tight, threading them up into a bundle at the nape of her neck. The braids reminded me of the way Linda's little brother's python looked when I watched it squeeze a mouse to death, a stack of rippling coils. Her dress rippled too, shrinking into her body as it dried, marking out the curve of her spine.

'What's it like, having a boyfriend?'

'It's all right.'

'I've never had a boyfriend,' she said, which wasn't exactly a surprise.

'Me and Liam met playing spin the bottle, but we haven't done anything yet.'

'Spin the bottle?' She brushed earth off the soles of her feet and threaded her toes into her tights.

'Yeah, you know. When you spin an empty bottle and then you have to kiss the person it lands on. Before Liam I had to snog this weird guy called Wiggy. He had manic hair, you know, and his mouth was all cold inside, like he'd been eating ice-cream, except he hadn't. Creepy.'

'I've never eaten ice-cream. I'm not allowed.'

'Wow,' I said, stupidly.

'I'm sorry about your brother.'

I nodded, not trusting myself to speak.

'What was his name?'

'Dylan.'

'That's nice. Does it mean something?'

'He was named after a poet.' I pushed myself up and stared out over the water so she couldn't see my face. 'I heard Laura Evans's Mam say it happened 'cause of his name, 'cause if you call your kid after a poet he's bound to end up either a suicide or a drunk.'

She was silent, lacing up her shoes.

'I'm named after a saint,' I said, my voice getting all croaky again. 'Which is kind of funny, if you think about it.'

I felt her take a step towards me, heard the brush of the ferns as she moved.

'I am a saint,' she said.

I wasn't sure I'd heard her right. 'Excuse me?'

'I have to get back to my little sister. She's just a bairn.'

'I can't call you Julian,' I shouted, to her back, as she climbed up the mountainside. 'It's a boy's name. And there's already a Julian in our year.'

She turned, clutching onto fern fronds for balance. Her face glimmered palely against her black dress.

'Call me Juliana, then,' she said. 'If you must.'

There was some tittle-tattle in town, about the Donnellys. Half-hearted, mostly, 'cause they were outsiders and scandal about the neighbours was juicier, more satisfying. I hadn't listened before, too immersed in my own problems, but now I drank it up. I loitered dangerously in the Happy Shopper, a Curly Wurly tucked into my waistband and a pineapple pencil top down my bra, and listened to Mrs Evans and Old Jeanie batting gossip back and forth across the counter like a ping-pong ball.

The Donnellys were English, from up north, Sunderland or Newcastle, somewhere where they say pet all the time. They were some funny religion too. Evangelicals, Mrs Evans speculated, but they didn't look that happy-clappy to me. They'd moved into the old cottage at the end of Millicent Street, the only house in town that wasn't joined to another. The mother and the two little boys – twins they looked like – were blonde and sullen-looking, pale as ghosts. The father had squinty eyes, the same rhubarby hair as Juliana, and was rumoured to sell bibles or vacuum cleaners in Swansea, out of the boot of his Morris Minor. And there was a baby, too. A little girl.

'Quick, quick. They're melting.'

Juliana laughed when she saw me scooting down the slope on my backside with a choc-ice in each hand. I liked the sound of her laughing. The choc-ices were cheapy ones from the Happy Shopper with fake chocolate covering. I paid for them with Mam's biscuit tin money 'cause I didn't want to send Juliana to hell with stolen ice-cream. They survived the walk pretty well, stuffed in my bag between two bottles of frozen Ribena.

Juliana took a bite of a half-melted choc-ice, chocolate smearing across her lips, and gasped. 'It hurts.'

She started laughing, again, and put a hand to her temple, getting a smudge of pale yellow ice-cream in her hair. She rolled her tongue over her teeth to warm them up. There was that flash again, of red on her palm, and she turned her hands away from me.

Walking back, alone by the river, I saw hundreds of tiny spiders in a square of sunlight, swinging backwards and forwards on their silk like trapeze artists. It had rained a bit, during the night, and raindrops stuck to the webs like lucky charms.

I walked down by the old cottage on Millicent Street once. She was standing in the little garden, the one they'd had to clear all the empty cider bottles out of when they moved in. The baby was crawling over cracked paving stones. She had a halo of wispy red hair, just the same colour as Juliana's.

'Hello Juliana,' I said.

'Get in the house, Maggie.' The voice was a man's, mild and casual.

I hadn't even noticed her father, leaning on the Morris Minor smoking a cigar. A little tremble passed across Juliana's shoulders. She knelt, not acknowledging me, and gathered the baby into her arms. Then she kissed that little baby on the forehead with such love and tenderness it made me feel like crying.

'Gracie, pet, it's time to come inside and play,' she said.

A sick rush of jealousy I couldn't explain flooded into my guts. Juliana stepped through the door with the baby and pulled it closed behind her. I stared at the peeling white paint. Juliana's father strolled around the side of the car, puffing smoke rings into the sky. There was a faint scent of vanilla in the air.

'Leave her alone, girl,' he said to me, still in that mild tone of voice. 'Leave her alone.'

He stubbed his cigar out on the garden wall with a single, vicious twist. It left a burn mark the size of a penny on the brick.

I kicked off my trainers and tip-toed around the shallows, getting the hems of my jeans wet. Juliana was floating on her back, sculling around in circles.

'I brought shampoo,' I said, holding up the bottle. 'The coconutty one.'

She stood up in the water. 'I can't take it home. My Dad would go mad.'

'We'll do it here, then.'

I walked into the pool, my wet clothes shrinking into my body. Juliana bent her knees, leant back, water lapping around her ears. I let the plastic shampoo bottle float, twisted her hair into a spiral, squeezed the water out. She closed her eyes and I felt her breath slow. I massaged shampoo through her hair, building up the lather, starting with the roots, kneading my fingers into her scalp.

She murmured something I couldn't hear, hesitated, breathed. 'I am Julian,' she said, with her eyes still closed, 'I asked for and was granted three graces of God's gift. Passion, sickness and three wounds.'

I smoothed more shampoo in, parting the tangles. Suds frothed up on the surface of the water.

'I saw the face of Christ.'

Her voice was so soft and dreamy I shivered.

'His face was beautiful… vivid. I touched him, and I made him bleed.'

Her eyelids were pale, almost transparent, fluttering like butterfly wings. I watched them, repeating her words under my breath. *Vivid.* I knew what it meant, of course, but I'd never heard anyone use it in conversation. It's what she was, *vivid*, lying there in the water with coconut shampoo frothing around her rhubarb hair. I started to rinse the shampoo out, sweeping her hair through the water in gentle waves.

'A terrible sickness fell upon me,' she whispered, 'when I was thirty and one half years old. I thought I would die. But I wanted to live. I wanted to live so badly, that I might love Christ more and understand his passion.'

'Hold your breath,' I said, stroking away the last of the shampoo from her hairline. I cupped water in my palms and splashed it across her face, washing the suds from her temples. I put my fingers in the hollow at the base of her skull and pushed up, her face breaking through the water.

'All done,' I said. 'Did you live or did you die?'

Juliana stood, a strand of her hair catching and pulling beneath the quick of my thumbnail.

'I lived,' she said, her breath like a ghost against my cheek. 'And was granted sixteen visions of God's love and compassion. It was a revelation of Christ's most divine love.'

She smiled, but the smile wasn't for me. It was like she wasn't there in the waterfall pool any more. Then she looked at me with her fern green eyes. 'Teleri, does my hair smell of coconut now?'

I leant in close, my nose bumping against her ear. Underneath the coconut, her scalp smelt of the forest. Leaves, earth and rain.

Juliana was undoing her buttons. Wading out deeper, to where the waterfall gurgled and foamed. She tugged her dress over her head, flung it off and it drifted away. She pulled her hair up, her back thin and white. She turned and I heard my breath catch and fade. A line of circular scars, about the size of pennies, ran from the hollow at the base of her throat, between her breasts, past her belly button, down into the water. There was another line, like a string of beads, threaded along the length of her collar bone, and when she lifted her shoulders I realised the scars ran across her arms, too, from the centre of one palm to the other. I went to Sunday school when I was little and we had hot cross buns at Easter, so I knew what the scars represented. It was a crucifix, painted onto her body with wounds.

'They're a blessing from God,' she said. 'So that I might more vividly perceive Christ's suffering.'

'Do they hurt you?'

'Sometimes.'

Her nipples were palest, palest pink, tiny wet shells. Not like mine, which were the colour of milk chocolate.

'How do they happen?' I whispered.

She didn't answer. And she didn't pull away when I brushed my fingertips along her collarbone, although I could tell from her eyes it was painful for her. The wounds were different ages, some new, red and raw, others faded and rough. I traced the path of scars with my fingers and still she didn't flinch, just stood there passively, water splashing onto her curved belly. I could see her red fluff, blurred by the water.

There were other scars on her belly and hips. Not stigmata, but fissures of silvery lines that reminded me of the circus of money-spiders flying through the light with raindrops on their silk. I ran my thumb across the web, the lines soft and velvety, and she did pull away then, with a faint clicking noise in the back of her throat, doubling over in the water and pulling her arms in, so that the line of the crucifix was broken.

'I'm sorry,' I said, 'I didn't mean to hurt you.'

She smiled at me, then, a gentle sweet smile, like the one she'd given baby Grace. 'Let me wash your hair, Teleri.'

When she pushed me forward, face down in the water to wet my hair, the weight of her breasts fell against my back, pressing my wet T-shirt and bra strap into my skin.

'Is Dyl in heaven, do you think?' I asked her, later, when we were sitting on a log in our wet clothes and watching pond skaters skim across the water.

'I don't know,' she said. 'I don't know everything.'

Then she kissed me. Just leant over, took my face in her hands, and kissed me. Her lips were swollen, moving against mine. She put her tongue in my mouth and I could taste that deep, earthy, woody scent, mixed in with metal and adrenalin. It was different from when I kissed Liam, softer, slower. More vivid. I felt her breath quicken and deepen, in time with mine. She pinched my lower lip between her teeth for a moment, before letting me go.

She shuffled on the log, getting comfortable, pressing her lips together.

'Well,' she said, matter-of-factly, 'your mouth's not cold at all.'

I burst out laughing, and after a bit she joined in. We laughed until we were crying. Crying properly, I mean. She took my hand.

'You're my best friend, Teleri,' she said.

I was her only friend. We both knew that, but it meant something that she'd said it.

She had to leave, to get home to Grace. At the top of the slope she kissed me again, a sweet, closed-mouth kiss this time. I watched her laughing, in the long second before the ferns sprang back, the sun fizzing off her wet hair. Then the valley folded in around her and she was gone. I didn't see her again.

Infinity

Sheena Brabazon

There are no adjectives in infinity, so the boy could not know himself.
He was. It was not enough. He wanted to see himself – to know whether
he was beautiful or not. The desire inside his belly grew into a fearsome
thing, scrabbling to escape. It was then that he built the Hall of Mirrors.

The hall was large and hexagonal, housing mirrors of every kind. He did
not know which of them distorted his image and which did not. He
would never know, but such was his need to look that even a falsely
fashioned version of himself was acceptable to feed his belly's desire. He
had created light in here, because infinity is bereft of it. It stung his eyes
at first, but they eventually became accustomed to it, banishing the
dancing spots of colour that floated before his retinas. He did not want
to look, he wanted to *see*, and so the mirrors reflected adjectives into the
empty space between themselves and the boy.

★ ★ ★

'Dead? No. You're wrong.'

Gabrielle didn't break down at the news. It was not true.

'I'm sorry, Mrs Donnat.' The young policewoman who'd
brought the news was out of her depth, and the back-up policeman
asked whether he could get Gabrielle a cup of tea. It sounded like a
foreign language. Dead. Tea.

The policewoman sat down beside her and held one of
Gabrielle's hands in two of her own.

'She's been identified by the school friend who was with her.
She had a library card and some other things on her with her name and
photo on them.'

The words did not reach Gabrielle's ears by the usual route. The
air molecules refused to transmit them, affronted by their message.

Instead they reached her underwater, and through layers of dense smog. She could barely make them out.

'She's at the cinema.'

The back-up policeman asked whether there was anyone they could phone who could come over; she shouldn't be alone. Stupid man. She wouldn't be alone, Claire would be home soon.

The policewoman had gone ahead and made her a cup of tea, which she pressed into Gabrielle's numb hands. Tea. Dead.

The warmth of the liquid travelled through the cup and began to dissolve the numbness in her. First in her fingers and toes, then along her limbs towards her chest. It was replaced by violent stabbing pains that robbed Gabrielle of her breath. She watched detached as her heart smashed to the floor and bled into the carpet. Then the screams began.

★ ★ ★

Tariq tenderly brushed back a stray hair from the girl's forehead.

'There,' he said. 'That's better.'

The girl did not respond.

He picked up some large medical shears from off the trolley next to him and commended them to his god and hers. He cut into her sternum and opened up her chest. Gently he removed her heart from its reluctant entanglement of arteries. It was not a small heart; she had been big for her age. She was, Tariq thought, as old as his own daughter. Twelve.

He took her heart to the set of scales designed to weigh death impartially, and noted down the results. He measured it and laid it out for examination, then returned to the body.

No longer a child, but not yet a woman, the girl's breasts had been beginning to take form underneath the elastic skin of youth, announcing to the world that the transition into adulthood had begun. It would never be completed. Tariq was not sad for the girl, who he prayed would be walking with God by now, but he had seen her mother and had heard her cries. He remembered the tortured noises his own mother had made when his brother had died. Long, lamentable, drawn-out wails that must have shaken the very foundations of heaven. People told her that time would heal her pain, but it had only taught her to function in spite of it. Tariq understood the sharp piercing caused by jagged shards of grief. Even now he sometimes called his brother's name, expecting him to come in by the door. The living, he knew, exist in turmoil, but the dead are at peace.

'Liver next,' Tariq explained to the girl. He treated each of the bodies in this way. Honourably. Caring. The way he would want his own children's bodies to be treated. He often questioned whether he was a good father; whether he gave his daughter and sons what they needed. Only a good father would question himself so relentlessly, his wife told him. He should concentrate more on being a good husband and empty the bins, she smiled.

The girl's organs were laid out in a row now. Her heart, liver, spleen, pancreas, kidneys and brain. All parts of what she had been, but not who she was. A human being could only be measured by his or her kindness, Tariq knew. By how they chose to behave. And only God could measure them.

The pathologist took only a cursory look at the organs. The girl had not died under suspicious circumstances and so there was little to do. He did not ask for tissue samples. The car had knocked her down and she had died. He recorded it on her chart in medical terminology, and gave Tariq the go-ahead to replace the organs.

Claire. That had been the girl's name when she had still needed one. Tariq used it when he blessed the needle and thread before he sewed up the gaping flaps of flesh along her chest and neck. He touched her cheek as softly as a calm breeze, and asked God to have mercy on her and her family, and to protect his own.

★ ★ ★

The brick thundered against the shop window propelled by a volatile force of hatred and alcohol. The strengthened glass crunched at the point of impact and spread out a spider web of cracks from its centre. Ruhal pushed his wife under the counter and told her to stay down.

'Go home, fucking Paki's!' the brick-thrower shouted. The woman with him hoisted her skirt and mooned Ruhal through the window. Another man picked up stones and began hurling them at the unyielding door, screaming abuse. Frustrated by the stones' lack of impact, he began furiously kicking at the window, while the brick-thrower aimed his missiles at a nearby street lamp, and the woman pissed on the pavement outside the shop's entrance. Ruhal's heart pushed at his ribcage, urging the bones to let it escape to somewhere safe.

'I'm calling the police!' he shouted through the door, phone in hand. He was answered by a barrage of insults and laughter. Then there was quiet.

'Have they gone?' Fatima asked.

'I don't know. You should stay hidden.'

Fatima rose to her feet. 'I am tired of hiding. I am tired of dogs' doings through the letter box, and scrubbing bad words off the door. I am so tired.'

Ruhal nodded, shamed that he could not protect his family better. He began to dial 999, but Fatima restrained his dialling hand.

'No,' she said. 'Call Tariq. I need to know that he is safe.'

'First the police, then Tariq,' Ruhal compromised. Fatima let go of his hand. It was illogical, she knew, to worry that her son was in danger because she was, but her mind would not be calmed until she *knew* he was all right.

The police would come as soon as they had an officer available. Ruhal had heard it many times before. It would be a long night. Tariq wanted to come over straight away, but he understood that his father's pride could not sustain such a blow. Ruhal believed that a man must be responsible for his own wife and children. Tariq would come tomorrow, then, and help with scrubbing the pavement and boarding up the window.

Fatima set about tidying up the shop; sorting out the rows of chocolate bars and cans of curried chicken. Ruhal knew better than to stop her. Her mind and hands needed an occupation.

'They will come again,' she said to her husband.

He wanted to say no, they wouldn't, but he knew it wasn't true. He didn't know when they would come, but they would certainly be back. They were like dogs returning to their own vomit. And if not them, then others. At first his anger had been directed only at them – when the children were small and it was still new. Now he saved it for those who did nothing. The people who said 'what a shame' and adopted sad expressions, then went on with their lives and ignored it all.

The window rattled loudly and Ruhal's breath was locked in his chest by a wave of adrenalin. A dog. Just a stray dog pushing up against the glass, searching for food and warmth. He exhaled, dizzy with pins and needles, and looked over to check that Fatima was all right. She stood frozen at the bottom of the narrow aisle holding a bottle of ketchup, silently crying. Ruhal did not ask why. He followed her gaze to the dog and back, then without speaking, unlocked and opened the door. The animal automatically backed away from him, tail between its legs, shivering with fear. Ruhal remained still. Eventually, driven by hunger greater than its fear, the dog sniffed at his shoe, then quickly retreated again. Twice more, until it finally dared enter the shop. Fatima had already emptied a can of dog food onto a saucer for it. It swallowed it almost immediately then sat, no longer shivering.

'That's right,' Fatima told it, holding out a hand to be sniffed. 'You're safe now.'

★ ★ ★

The boy saw the adjectives reflected in the mirrors, and still he did not know whether he was beautiful or not. Frightened; caring; joyful; hopeless; empty. Instead of calming the desire in his belly, the words fed it and made it grow. He did not understand why he continued to stare, but he could not look away. Each word was reflected back at itself in a thousand other mirrors, which changed it each time, until it was something other than itself. The boy may have been beautiful, but the mirrors and the lights made it impossible to tell.

Ramshackle

Zoe Lambert

The first time I realised I did not have to be good, I hid my hearing aids beneath my hair, climbed through a hole in Barlow High fence and spent the afternoon in Jim's garden. The five of us lay on the grass, which itched my legs and tickled sneezes in my nose. The garden was ramshackle with bushes, rusty spades, broken plant pots and edged with oak trees that mostly hid the high school roof. Robert and Jim sat cross-legged and mumbled so low I turned up the volume on my hearing aid, and then down again when it squealed because Ben was tuning his guitar, his ear tipped towards the sound and long fringe dangling.

Robert, Jim and Ben skipped school. They got away with it; they stringed A's like beads and spent their time sprawled here, strumming their guitars. Other lads - the ones from the council estate - got caught; they broke bottles and huddled outside newsagents where trouble blew towards them like empty crisp packets.

My friend Shannaz plaited her uncovered hair, stretched out on her headscarf, her legs peeping out of her long skirt. Shannaz's concentration on her split ends told me she was deciding on the tale to tell her parents when she came home late. She often hung out here and knew how to smoke. 'Come to Jim's,' she had signed to me, as we munched flapjacks at lunchtime. 'Robert will be there.' She was not bad at signing since her little sister had severe hearing loss (90dB) and went to a special needs school because of her behaviour - she screamed a lot and could shout 'fuck you' really well. If I was that deaf I'd get annoyed too. It was bad enough at 70 dB.

Shannaz had argued that it was only CDT and Mr McMundy wouldn't notice, since his glasses were always covered in sawdust. In other classes I sat at the front for my hearing and because I liked learning new things; I loved the satisfaction of completed sums and answers in full sentences. Last CDT lesson we'd both finished our design projects and the class was in chaos, so we started messing and inventing rude signs.

When Mr McMundy was not distracted by what the lads were doing with the hacksaw, he leant on our desk, holding the microphone to his mouth. I switched my body aid back on. I'd turned it off because he talked to himself in the storeroom, and I didn't really want to know. 'Come on Mary,' he said. 'This silly behaviour isn't what I'd expect of *you*.' He smiled a pitying thin-lipped smile, as if my sudden silliness at least gave me character.

At lunch I'd stared at the hole in the fence that seemed to have been gnawed by a large rat, imagining myself slipping through it, running out the other side. I pictured Robert and me chatting about music for hours, every word clear. In class I only dared to give him quick stares over my shoulder, even when all I could see was his brown shoulder length hair that was sometimes silky, but often stringy.

Now I was here. Robert and Jim were talking about a band. The sounds of the words sailed past my ears. My eyes flicked from one to the other, but it's hard to speech read in a group and I couldn't make out which band they meant because of the guitar. People don't realise that hearing aids amplify sound. They don't clarify it.

'What, you like The Sugar Babes?' I asked.

'No, Mary. Sonic Youth,' said Robert and laughed. 'So-nic Youth,' he repeated slowly, picking up a CD case next to him. I could feel myself blushing as I watched his lips: they were round and full, with dry patches.

'They're… playing… Academy… I said… Do you like them?'

'Me?'

But they had their heads turned to each other. Their hair looked greasier than ever and fell in their faces. Robert thought I didn't get music, just like everybody else outside Jim's garden. I wriggled myself closer. I wanted to tell them I could play 'Smells like Teen Spirit' on a keyboard. I loved music, especially loud songs. I'd turn up the volume on my earphones, or hold my ear next to the speaker till it hurt. I searched for the phonics in words when I half heard them. I'd shout them in my bedroom and repeat them in my head. Words were bright, sharp things, which crunched and tingled amidst my memories of sound from before my ear infections: the creak of a door opening, the rustle of a wrapper.

I gave up on the band names. Picking the grass, I blinked through itchy-watery eyes at the back door of Jim's huge house, which I imagined was stuffed with books and lost shoes, where light from curved windows picked out dust swimming in the air. Mine was boxy with skinny walls, and even I switched off my hearing aids because of the neighbours' non-stop Kylie.

Mum must have sensed I was skipping school. She always seemed to know what I was up to. I checked my mobile, but there were no messages. Every day she texted me kisses from her office. Sometimes I really wished she would find a boyfriend.

Ben, who had undone most of the buttons on his blue school shirt, was smoking an overweight cigarette. He passed it to me.

'It's a spliff,' Shannaz signed. I held it carefully in my hand, the heat between my fingers. I inhaled like Audrey Hepburn, but it scorched my throat and in my nose. I coughed, tried not to, and was nearly sick. They were shaking their heads. Jim grinned and clapped me hard on my back. He told me to hold the smoke in my chest before breathing it out. Shannaz signed what he was saying, though I'd understood him perfectly. She giggled and rolled her eyes as I held my breath till it burned the back of my throat. *What can you expect? Did you think Mary could smoke?* her eyes said, as if we weren't friends at all. She took the spliff off me and rolled onto her back. Everybody lay down, so I did as well and pulled up the grass till I had a pile of it. I wondered what I was supposed to feel, other than nausea and a rushing in my head.

We lolled on our backs till I got goose bump legs, the sun settled between the trees and spidery shadows crept over the lawn. I could smell the grass I twisted between my fingers and a hint of the school canteen. I could definitely smell the mashed potato from lunch, even from this far away. Jim went inside, his arms and legs swinging widely as he walked, and returned with cans of Heineken and plastic glasses. He gave everybody a glass and Shannaz drank hers down in one gulp.

'Why the glasses?' I asked Jim, wishing he'd forgotten to pour me some. I didn't like beer.

'My mum says we can finish off the beer as long as we drink it in the glasses,' I speech read off him. My phone vibrated. 'WHERE ARE YOU?' mum had texted. 'I WAITED AT BUS STOP. WHAT ARE YOU DOING?' She liked to meet me and have a moment by moment account of my day. I used to think all mothers kept diaries about their children's growth and development, not just when they were babies. She got her own audiometer off eBay and measured my hearing every month, even though sensorineural hearing loss can't be cured. She has a 'Mary's Hearing Chart' on the bathroom wall. Another text bleeped.

'WHY AREN'T YOU REPLYING??'

I swigged some horrible beer and turned off my phone. I bit my lip. Mum would be worried.

Jim crawled towards me. He reached over and pushed my hair behind my ear and lightly touched my aid. I blinked at him in surprise. He was the wrong one. I looked over at Robert, but he was just strumming away. Jim was staring at my right cheek. Perhaps I was blushing. He leaned in and I thought, 'That's it. My first kiss, but from the wrong one.'

His fingers brushed my cheeks and pinched it hard. Then he fell back on the grass, laughing, lifted his legs in the air and kicked them. I stared at him in confusion. I looked for Shannaz. She was busy kissing Ben in a heap of school shirts and long black hair. She'd never said there was something between them. I wondered why I was there. I brushed my hair back over my ears and rubbed my sore cheek. For once I wasn't being good. I'd truanted, smoked, sipped beer (though I'd been pinched instead of kissed) and yet I was bored. Was I destined just to study for my GCSEs?

Wrapping my arms round my knees, I realised I was in my own head. I liked this. I slowly moved my head from side to side, feeling its weight. Everybody else was outside it. Before, I'd felt trapped in silence, but I was in my skull and it was fine. I didn't belong in this garden, with this group. That was fine too.

'Shannaz!' I called. But she didn't hear me. Grabbing my bag and coat, I walked to the gate, sure they wouldn't notice; Jim was still on his back with his legs in the air and Robert was going for it on the guitar.

I walked back to school. It was all closed up, not even the caretaker was around. Not even the cleaners. I squeezed through the hole in the fence and skirted the prefabs to the yard. It was eerie without anybody there; the classrooms looked dark, the shadows were all wrong. I could almost feel Year Seven running round me, their ghosts swishing and pushing past. I could nearly see the shapes and lines of where the different groups of girls huddled. I'd be leaving here soon. I wasn't sure what I'd do. The careers teacher avoided my desk and just smiled when I wrote down 'florist' in the 'My Career' box. It was quiet in a florist's and I quite liked the word. Though I was not keen on flowers, so perhaps it was not such a good idea. The wind swept my hair up and I held onto my skirt. I felt the gravel with the toe of my shoe then I ran to the gate, but it was locked. I sped round the school and climbed through the hole in the fence. Gasping for breath, I ran down the road, past the big old houses on one side and the beginnings of the council estate on the other. I headed to the bus stop and remembered that I was not being good today. But it's hard not being good when you are on your own. I wasn't sure what I wanted to do, other than not go home. So I walked down the road and made for the shops, even though I knew they'd be closed.

Shooting Jelly with a Shotgun

Adam Maxwell

'Ow! Shit! I think a bee stung my ear!'

'Fucking hell, Charlie. Your ear's bleeding!'

'What? Oh my God!'

Charlie passed out before I reached him. As I approached his crumpled body I could see the widening crimson patch seeping through the fibre of his T-shirt. I gagged, I admit it. I doubled over, my hands grabbing my knees and my eyes closed. An icy sweat climbed up my back and as I opened my eyes I could see a chunk of Charlie's ear lying a couple of feet away.

Becoming a victim of a stray nail from a careless carpenter's nail gun changed Charlie. The realisation that if the nail had been two inches to the left he could have lost an eye, or worse. He had been working as a bricklayer on a couple of contracts with me, and would never wear a hard-hat, instead preferring his own brand of lax sloppiness. Now he slept in the fucking thing. Losing half an ear will do strange things to a man.

A few weeks later we had a job laying foundations. Me and Charlie were on a break and without any warning, he was catapulted backwards across the site in a puff of masonry dust.

For a moment I just stared at the space he had just occupied. There were little specs of dust floating downwards. It was then my mind began processing the accompanying noise.

It had sounded like someone shooting a jelly with a shotgun and then a split second later a sledgehammer hitting a porcelain toilet.

Everyone knows that bones break when they're hit too hard, they're weak under extreme pressure and can splinter and break as easily as twigs.

Bones, however, are not dead wood. Every cell in your body is constantly being replaced by new living tissue and your bones are no different. At the hospital later that day I was surprised when the doctor told me that the pelvis is made up of three bones that grow together as people age; the ilium, ischium and pubis. On each side of the pelvis there is a hollow cup, the acetabulum, which serves as a socket for the hip joints.

I turned to look behind me. Charlie lay, a concrete block embedded between his splayed legs, separating his ilium from his ischium and his pubis from his acetabulum. The doctors later told me his hips had both been pushed out of socket as his pelvis shattered.

It got worse.

His poor mangled pelvis had absorbed the majority of the blow and had cracked just like the breaking porcelain toilet sound which had echoed around the building site. It troubled me all the way to the hospital when I found out what the other sound was.

It is a fairly well known fact in most circles that if a man is kicked between the legs then the results will be pain, shock, confusion and sometimes even nausea. Kick hard enough and you can tag vomiting and an inability to walk to the list. The blood vessels which supply the testicles through the hole in the middle of the pelvis will burst and begin to bleed internally into the scrotum.

If, for argument's sake, a large concrete block swings loose and strikes you between the legs, doctors will tell you that a testicular rupture may occur. This is when the testicle is compressed against the pubic bone with such force that the testicle is crushed against the bone and as Charlie lay there, passed out and vomiting, I could feel my hairs standing on end. It was like on some spiritual level his balls were calling out to mine.

The doctors will tell you this. What they won't tell you is that it sounds like shooting jelly with a shotgun.

Cord

Mario Petrucci

She burst into the attic room just as he was looping the cord through its hoop at the apogee of the ceiling's V. Without a glance her way, instantly, he tried to hide the end of the cable behind him, as if the rest of its bright red length were not in plain view as he went limp, head, hands, neck, as though a headmistress had just walked in on a very silly boy and caught him there in his schoolboy shorts standing on the janitor's ladder and he knew no excuse would ever do yet folded behind his back the irrefutable proof that he had been tying and showing off some kind of obscene knot.

'Oh god. *Oh* god…' The tendons in her neck pulled sideways with such force that it seemed the pillar of a suspension bridge was thrust outwards from her blouse. In each hand she gripped an upright of the stepladder as though, in some appalling way, she were about to steady it.

'Leave me alone. Please.'

'Just like that? What the fuck, Tom? What?'

'Please…'

She began to shake the ladder. He tried to keep his balance, knew how silly he must look. More from embarrassment than anything else he came down and half-collapsed, half-sat on the bottom step, head in hands. It looked nothing like a co-ordinated movement, more a clumsy grope towards gravity. He seemed to be trying to speak without using any muscles, without taking breath.

'Please. Want to. Please.' She had no sense of how long she sat there next to him, afraid to move. Him, just an arched back trying to breathe, charged with bad electricity that crackled *Don't touch. Just don't ever touch.*

Somehow they went downstairs together. She slung one arm around his waist and made him walk. As if every painstaking step might be a hope. Muscles moving. Another beat of his heart. Another whimper. All of it Life. Life, and not its terrible final opposite. He stood at the sink, shoulders and chest collapsed, head down, and began to moan. His nape, exposed at the angle of pity. What could she do? All her resources fell short of this. This wasn't her mother's war, with the brewing of sweet hot tea after the bombs fell, after families were ripped apart and left flapping with great irretrievable gapes in them. This was something he actually wanted. Nothing put it right. Not holding him, or talking all night with him, or making love to him, or making tea. And still she had reached for the kettle the second they stepped into the kitchen's white fluorescence, as though somehow with its soft smell of bread and coffee that room was safer than the rest, as if the hiss of cold water and the comforting gargle of the kettle's hot throat might tap into her dead mother's strength. And yes, she stepped up to him and held him. 'Let me do it,' he said. 'I want to go.'

'Oh Tom…' That was all she had. A name. Even as she clung to him she knew he was out there somewhere else. His name was a thin cord coiled around her arms, an umbilicus of rope strung out from her spit of sand across a huge swell, with him too far out, her foothold dissolving, his dark blot facing the wrong way into a powerful outward current. That familiar small sound – half play, half mantra – as heavy now as yanking on half a mile of drenched rope. But here he was, close and warm. 'Tom *please*.' She muttered it hard into his chest, hands clasped against his spine. Felt him tighten, keep her out. She spoke with her lips pressed to his shirt, pressing for flesh and blood, believing they might hear her, that she might speak directly to his body, his heart.

'Make that tea.'

It was not her words that called him back, but that definite *click* and green light from the small lighthouse of the kettle. She stepped back from him half a pace, opened at last a space between them. A thread of spittle from her mouth hung there in the chasm an instant, suspended its tiny bead of mercury for a moment, then vanished. She had her back to the kitchen and was lifting the second heaped teaspoon into the tannin-stained pot when she heard the door jolt and click behind her. She ran across the room, tea leaves stinging into her eyes and tickling down her breasts. The handle wouldn't open. She heard his deliberate tread back up the stairs, the scraping readjustment of the stepladder. The slight squeak as he pressed his weight onto its first step.

In slow motion she fell against the door. Slid down it face-first onto her knees. Through her cheek she felt its firm inches of obdurate resistance, its obstinate wooden self. *God. Please. Let it melt for her, splinter*

for her. Let it know her. Part, and let her through. Please. It was as though a
voice spoke from somewhere else, outside her head. But the fibres
remained close-knit as surely as for any thief or murderer. Then it rose
in her. Now she thought only with her fists as first they beat then
punched the door, as she stood and leant into it, lashing out at its shiny
brass coat-hook, the classy silver handle. Wood and metal picked up
specks of ochre then a sticky smear of bright blood as she pummelled
and kicked, smashed her forehead against the relentless planks, felt her
left shoe split and fly, tasted the hot tang as a tooth broke in her enlarging
mouth, as her entire body flung itself at the closed world, this shut fuck
of a wooden mouth, this mouth, her mouth growing into one vast
bloodied drawn-out bellowing sound... *TOM!* She heard the crash of
the stepladder as it fell, saw in her mind's X-ray his heels dangling there
just a few feet the other side of the ceiling, kicking and twitching, and
she fell too, into a hopeless silent sob, the creases of her squeezed-shut
eyes, her drawn-back lips, merging and dissolving into the expression
made so that no one born of this earth, no one with a grain of feeling
or compassion, could ever look upon such a face and remain detached.

The door clicked open behind her and she sank onto her back,
supine to the light, saw the stairs leading to the attic, the landing light-
bulb swinging on its cord, all the half-shadows and angles of the hallway
swaying crazily, as if the house itself were reeling from immense impact.
Or laughing. Then his face slid into view, upside-down over hers. He saw
her face frozen, like a terrible death-mask cemented forever in a spasm
of broken grief. 'Do it Tom. Just fucking do it. Do us both. Fucking *die.*'

Slowly he slumped to the floor, sat near her with his back
against the stairs. With great fatigue he loosened the scarlet cable from
his neck, leaving behind another, almost its twin, scored deep into his
skin. From the twisted cord, where it had snapped, the blue, brown and
electric green strands of the cable sprang like stunted shoots. Flecks of
copper glinted there in the rocking light from the landing. 'Couldn't
even do this right,' he whispered hoarsely. 'Maybe time I tried something
else. Fucking British cable...'

And they began to laugh. She, chuckling at first, then he joining
in, building a ladder of coughs and gasps, filling the house with a rocking
swaying splitting sound, passing the joyless hack back and forth, forth and
back, until the old man next door having overheard all the various
commotions – that stooped stump of a man who had seen off two wives
and two wars, whose body was a fretwork of pain and inconvenience,

who often thought of chewing some of the old bitter green stuff and lying down once and for all with the rats – cocked his white head and considered how, with all the crash-bang-wallop of their love-making, and with all this raucous laughter, how happy a couple they must be.

Falling Out of the Sky

Penny Feeny

Paris, Frankfurt, Geneva, Helsinki, Rome. Other people knew cities by their fine monuments, parks or palaces. Miller knew them by the shape of their sprawl: a dog chasing its tail, a ship capsized, a hunchback curled in a heap. At night the patterns of lights would rise to greet him like old friends, like gemstones glittering in a necklace or the rings winking on Anna's fingers.

Since the accident – the incident as the Italians would say – he'd kept thinking of Anna. Flying low over Rome he imagined her sunbathing naked on her terrace, looking up at the shadow he'd traced across her square of blue sky. On arrival at Leonardo da Vinci, a few hours to fritter, he'd made an impulsive phone call. She had recognised his voice immediately. 'My God, Miller!' And the thrill of it had taken him back to their fierce encounters in late-night drinking clubs, hotel bedrooms, steamy cafes, around the world. Nowadays he shared bland functional lodgings with his co-pilots: emptying the mini-bar, flicking through satellite TV channels, keeping an eye out for other card players – no language barriers in a hand of poker.

'Would it be okay,' he asked. 'If I come by?'

'Sure, I never go anywhere these days.'

'I didn't know if you'd still be around.' Alone, he meant.

'Just me and my brood.' Adding with her throaty laugh: 'I've turned into Catwoman, darling.'

They used to be all over the place, he remembered from his earlier visits to the city. Hordes of cats – black, white, ginger, tortoiseshell, tabby; battle-scarred scavengers stalking the ruins of the Forum, basking on a warm patch of mosaic, sheltering under a fallen Ionic column, giving birth on a pile of aromatic bay leaves. They'd gone now.

Outside the apartment block, Miller hesitated. He hadn't seen her for years. Even now he wasn't quite ready to acknowledge the string of circumstances that brought him to her door. An old girlfriend, he'd told the rest of the crew casually. Used to be a model, retired young and wealthy. Always a free spirit. Back in those days flying had made him feel like God. How could it have diminished to a job as dull and familiar as an old pair of shoes?

Until recently, that is. A bundle of rags, propped against the peeling stucco of the building, not far from his feet, shifted, extended a hand. Miller, dismissing the image of that other bundle, the broken bag of bones for which he felt responsible, quickly rang Anna's bell. Logic told him that of course he wasn't a murderer. But it couldn't stop him feeling like one.

There was no lift to her top floor apartment. Miller was breathing heavily by the time he reached the final flight of stairs. She was waiting for him in the doorway with the light behind her, so he couldn't see the lines on her face or the silver threading her hair. But the sinuous shape blocking the entrance – one hand on her hips, a cigarette drooping from the other – was as powerfully erotic as ever.

He had planned to embrace her, but she moved swiftly back through the corridor, leading him onto her terrace. 'Of course I'm pleased to see you,' she said. 'But I think you should know that I've given up men.'

The terrace wrapped around her tiny apartment was a jungle of vines and bougainvillea, tall rustling forests of bamboo prowled by miniature tigers. Anna pushed back a swathe of foliage. 'See,' she threw at him over her shoulder, 'Your world may be shrinking but mine's still growing.'

The sharp impatient blare of Roman traffic from the street below was overlaid with a soft hum that reminded him of the throb of a 747 at cruising speed. He identified the tumbling mumbling chorus as cats purring. They wrapped their quivering tails around Anna's brown legs and growled at Miller's trousers. She shooed a tabby off a table, picked up a carafe of wine and poured him a glass.

He shook his head. 'No thanks. I don't anymore.'

She looked briefly surprised. Possibly she was recalling the long brandy-fuelled nights when they had been lovers.

'Had a bit of liver damage from a bout of hepatitis.' No need to go into details; he'd got over it. 'Gave up the drink a few years ago.'

'And I've chosen celibacy! What a pair we are. Tell me, have you given up anything else?'

Wasn't that what he had always liked about Anna? Her ability to cut to the quick, to ask the questions others had either not thought of, or perhaps not dared to voice.

He sat on a spindly wrought-iron chair, felt it wobble beneath him. 'That's why I wanted to see you. This is probably going to be my last trip here. I'm quitting.'

They had never actually said goodbye. They'd simply drifted apart when he'd been taken off the European routes for a while. This was his chance to tie up the loose ends. He thought she'd probably understand. After all, she'd abandoned a successful career herself, had reduced her globe-trotting to a mass of potted plants that needed watering every night and flock of creatures that needed feeding every day. No wonder she couldn't leave home.

Anna no longer plucked her eyebrows into fine supercilious arcs; she brought them together in a frown. 'Why?' she asked.

Athens, Istanbul, Madrid, Naples, Nice, New York: a carousel of cities to pick and mix. Why on earth, Miller wondered, did people always want to talk to him about their holiday experiences?

Standing at the edge of a Christmas drinks party, gazing through the window at an overcast sky. Accosted by a woman with thick make-up and thicker ankles, determined to pass on the hell of being stuck in the lift in one of the towers of La Sagrada Familia. 'Midsummer! You have no idea of the smells! Mind you, when we finally did get to the top it was worth it. The views of Barcelona are quite incredible.'

'He probably knows that,' said her husband over her shoulder.

'Of course!' She giggled and gave Miller a playful poke in the ribs. 'Go on, say it for us now.'

'What?'

'This is your Captain speaking.'

Miller guffawed along with her husband, as if at a tremendous joke.

'We travel abroad at least six times a year, you know. We've been everywhere. I suppose you could say we pay your wages.'

'Can't we duck out next time,' Miller pleaded with his wife, Diane.

'I don't think showing your face once in a while is so much to ask.'

In fact, Diane had long ago created a social life in which he played very little part. Quite often, when he was home on leave, he found himself more of a hindrance than an asset to his family – an obstacle they fell over in the house because they'd forgotten he might be in the way. His teenage children had passed the stage where they were excited to have a father who flew aeroplanes. They knew he was little more than a taxi driver in gold braid. They'd already visited more exotic locations than they could count and prefered to hang out at home with their friends.

'It's not much of a perk, these days, your cheap travel entitlement,' said Diane. 'When flights are being sold at a penny a seat.'

'Would you rather I did something else?'

'Such as?'

'I could cash in the pension. Start up a business.'

She shrugged as if it was scarcely anything to do with her. 'It would be odd having you home all the time.'

Tel Aviv, Baghdad, Beirut, Kabul. He'd been on the Middle East run: shambolic, broken down cities, a different order of ruins. On the way out, the First Officer had been at the controls: Miller was trying to ease himself into a training role. On the way back from Kabul, he agreed to take over the landing at Heathrow. A clear dawn, visibility good, radio control efficient, the descent almost as automatic as the drive home to Twickenham. A slight lurch of the stomach he welcomed as he would welcome any indication that he still had feelings. Circling in a wide arc above the sprawl of the M4 corridor, lowering the wheels and the wing panels, he heard the roar and rush of metal slicing through the air. Ahead of him the runway, the long belt of tarmac he met with scarcely a judder. The passion had gone, but he could still effect a smooth landing.

'Heading straight home?' asked the First Officer.

'Yeah, probably. What day is it?'

'Thursday.'

'Thursday. Right.' Kids at school, he supposed. Wife at work. Sometimes he lost track. No point in hurrying. He might as well have breakfast in the canteen: black pudding and fried eggs. Lots of tea to give him energy. She'd have saved up a list of household jobs, Diane. She didn't like to think of him sitting around with nothing to do. He wished he found sleep easier. He wished that a legacy of night-flying and early calls didn't make it so hard for him to obliterate more than a few hours at a time. In the event, he remembered, he went home and dreamt of Anna.

The police turned up a couple of days later, on a Saturday afternoon. Diane pulled a brush through her hair and went to answer the door, her voice unusually high and querulous. Miller could hear them ask for him, just a few routine questions, they said, nothing to worry about. But their panda car in its shrieking livery was parked in the driveway and Diane would have to explain its presence to the neighbours. Her face, on being shut out of the chilly dining room, was thunderous.

The one who had flashed the badge of a Detective-Inspector said to Miller: 'We're investigating the death of a suspected asylum seeker.'

Miller urged them to sit at the table, wished he could have met them on neutral ground.

'We think he might have stowed away on your plane.'

'Jesus! What, in the baggage hold?'

'In the under-carriage. Behind the wheel shaft.'

'But that's impossible.'

'It's been done before.'

'What makes you think he was on my flight?'

'We can't be certain, but he seems to have been a Afghani. And the time fits.'

Miller rubbed his forehead in a daze. 'Where is he now?'

The second policeman spoke. 'A man walking his dog says he saw him fall. He landed in a field a few miles from here. Dead of course.'

A rattling in the corner caught their attention. Diane opened the hatch from the kitchen and poked through three cups of tea and a bowl of sugar. The doors of the hatch stayed open. The tea grew cold.

'I don't suppose you noticed anything?'

Miller had to make an effort to keep his voice down. 'For Christ's sake, what would I notice? A plane isn't like a car. You don't feel the thud when a dog runs into your bumper or a suitcase flies off the roof.'

'No? Well, we're having the security cameras at Kabul airport checked but there's not much else we can do.'

'Pretty useless sort of hijacking,' observed Miller. All he could see of Diane was a strip of pink sweater bulging around her waist.

'Wasn't a hijack, mate. Just some damn fool of a refugee thought he could cheat gravity.'

The body, they told Miller, had fallen frozen from the sky. As soon as it hit the ground it shattered. The Afghani had wrapped himself in layers of jackets, trousers and blankets – enough to survive the coldest temperatures he might have experienced so far in the ice covered mountains of his homeland. At 30,000 feet he had no hope of survival.

'You'd have thought the poor sods would have got the message by now,' said the Detective-Inspector.

Diane was ironing. The scent of clean freshly pressed laundry hovered at the edge of the room. Miller thought: How desperate must a man be?

Sitting in the sun on Anna's terrace while she brewed him an espresso. A distant view of the Colosseum, of a world lost two thousand years ago. A swift movement made him turn his head: a lizard helpless in the jaws of an elegant tortoiseshell. As he watched, the lizard's tail dropped to the ground, writhed once or twice. The cat bounded away with her prey.

Anna handed him a tiny brimming black cup. 'Is this how you like it?' Distracted, remote. Treating him like a stranger.

She had changed too. Her breasts sagged beneath her tee-shirt, her fingers were bare. She'd pawned her rings, she said, for vets' bills. Couldn't be bothered to redeem them. Miller nodded. He'd paid for at least two of those rings. He could still picture the jeweller in Amsterdam, eye grotesquely distorted through his lens, spreading out diamonds for Anna to choose. Diane preferred more practical gifts. Their home was stuffed with Murano glasses and Spanish paella dishes.

The strong coffee scalded his throat. 'I knew nothing about the guy who fell. No idea he was there. Why should I feel guilty?'

'I tell you, Italy's full of Albanians coming over any way they can. Swimming even.'

'I think there's one begging outside your portone.'

'*Chi se ne frega.* No-one gives a fuck.'

'Do you miss it?' he said suddenly.

Sex? Work? Travel? What was he really asking?

Anna tipped her face towards the sky, closed her eyes and spoke to the light froth of cloud. 'I had a baby who died,' she said.

'God, I'm sorry.' Miller's children were robust, disrespectful, increasingly independent.

'It was a while ago now. And it wasn't yours, if that's what you're thinking.' Her voice was smooth as chocolate, but her hands were balled into fists. A cat kneaded a hollow in her lap. 'Death makes you re-examine your life, wouldn't you say?'

'I don't know. I don't know anything any more.'

Anna straightened her fingers, tapped a cigarette from the pack but didn't light it.

'I'm sorry, Miller. I can't help you.'

He sighed, reached out and pulled her into his arms. He needed to hold her very tight one last time, to counter the thrust of her hips with his own, to stroke her long swan's neck; he'd even bear one of her ferocious temper-tantrums if it meant he could feel something again.

Anna stood passively in his grasp. There was no spark, nothing like the connection that had fired them in the old days. He kissed her cheek.

'It's been good to see you,' he said.

'Don't pretend you're going to keep in touch.'

'I've already said this is my last trip.' The fragrance of jasmine, the dance of sunlight on her skin as she broke free. His balls ached. Was that a good sign?

'Goodbye Miller,' said Anna.

He climbed slowly to the bottom of the building. The stairwell seemed particularly dark after the brightness of the terrace. Cobwebs massed in the corners of the old wooden ceiling. Spiders dangled perilously. He stepped outside the main door into the street. Overhead soared a flash of silver jet. Incredible, he thought, how empty the skies seemed from below. Like the world from above.

A cough and a shuffle made him look down. The Albanian was still crouched against the wall. Miller dug into his pockets, pulled out a fistful of euros he wasn't going to need any more and stuffed them recklessly into the man's hands.

Help Me

Penny Anderson

I know everything. I know it all. Ask me whatever you want – I have all the answers. I can do anything. I have complete control over my own destiny. My future rests in my own hands, and anything is possible.

But then I wonder. When I saw you, I began to wonder.

The round white boxes appeared overnight, called Emergency Information Points, placed on city centre walls, by busy main roads, next to bars. Installed by a council ever eager to help, they are studded with one red button. You press with a question and I have the answer, as I sit beside a closed-circuit screen, computers blinking competitively nearby. I answer all enquiries, my working world reduced to talking video heads, all spouting disembodied confusion.

'Help me,' you said.

You are a grey vision, your face is hidden, a hood pulled down, probably a vexatious junkie or just another smart aleck drunk. My reply was brief and harsh. 'Step away from the box. You are being filmed.'

But I saw you.

At first I wonder, and then I know. Truthfully, I have limited control, but I do know most of the answers. Really. I do.

The one that night had a body like the underside of a lobster, crustacean abs (one thousand sit-ups per day – no question). Despite his confidence, we barely shared a word and even though he never called, the memory alone made the day pass by fast. I hate Fridays. People are drunk by lunchtime:

'I'm soooo pissed!'

(*You're sooo funny.*)

'Hi! I'm American and…'

(*Oh yeah? And what am I supposed to do about that?*)

'I'm ugly, I've got no money, my life's a mess and I'm going nowhere.'

(*Aren't we all?*) 'Step away from the box…'

'Where the cash-point, please?'

'Just down the road.' (*Right next to you, stupid*).

'Help me,' you said, imploring now, that hood still obscuring your appearance

'Step away from the box, or you will face prosecution,'... (*May be prosecuted* – I correct my matronly pronouncement.) I don't believe you need my help. I don't believe I should help you. Anyway, you're gone.

But maybe I could help you, if I decided to listen.

'Help me? Please?' you asked, desperately. Now you sound genuine; in real need of assistance. You require information. Being as I dole out facts, and since I worship certainty, I can give you information.

The first one, you just get out of the way. It's worthless. Useless. They make you feel like a fragile porcelain car, and they're changing the spark-plugs and quickly checking the oil with a reedy, apologetic dipstick.

'Do you know the way to the library?'

(*Yes. I do. I know.*)

'Help me.' you said, next in line. Pleading now; demanding – not that begging will help. I suspect you might be just another pathetic loser.

Wednesday after work, one traced patterns on my flat belly, and we were drunk, and I asked him to leave. He was a tourist. No point in him staying really.

You were silent, and just stood, still in front of the camera. You never showed your face, but I knew you were in trouble.

Most of them were boring. So few were remarkable. I don't remember their faces, and as for the names – often I never got round to caring. One scared me though; whimpered about his soul being stained purple by the sin of fornication, and then cried quietly, forlorn in the dark, just like a tragic girl, and in his sleep asked for his mother.

'Help me,' you asked, back again, then gone in an instant.

Another was much older than me, well-preserved, tanned like leather, though with suspiciously blonde hair. At first I thought he was rich, but it was all sun-bed and a loan to get his eyes done. His wife had died, and he wanted to be 'Ian. Just Ian. Not Ian-who's-57...' He was the kind of boy who at school everyone thought would get rich or elected, except they never do. He was a caretaker. He was grateful.

One bar shuts, another one opens. They all feel just the same. On Sundays I rest, Mondays I wax, condition, polish and smooth.

Tuesdays – just a casual drink, no expectations. Wednesdays – I see what there is on offer. Thursdays – I'm serious about the task in hand, Fridays I'm always in demand, and Saturdays, I'm on the prowl again. I do want to travel though, but you seem different today – skittish, and I can't hear you breathe.

'Help me,' you say.

All I can do is refer you to an agency. I can send you to The Samaritans – they're close by, which always makes me laugh. 'Suicide City' my friend calls merry mancland. The Samaritans are right next to the Cornerhouse cinema. How ironic. So many culture lovers enjoy profound, wordy films about inconsolable Swedes, with sympathy just one step away.

'Help me,' you said.

We have so much in common, you and I. We both roll around Manchester like ball-bearings in a haunted pinball machine, banging into strangers, bumping into unforgiving walls, aware of the danger but too numb to escape, repelled and attracted by others, scared of drunks, and the journey home. Afraid of the revealing day, we make our moves by night. At closing time, we roam the loud and teeming streets, looking, both of us searching.

And somehow you expect me to help you. I'm just not sure if that's the right way round. It's funny, you know, and sometimes I wonder why, but at the moment, this is how I am: for some reason, of the all the people I meet, it's you I want to look in the eye.

I really need to look right into your eyes.

Do Something Good

Tom Palmer

Sam liked it when there was a war on. Footage of fighter planes, burnt-out buildings and sieges. Hours of debate on the television. And the war in Bosnia had it all.

At first it was enough watching the news at seven, nine and ten, then *Newsnight*. But after a while he needed more and had satellite installed for twenty-four-hour news. He'd just got the money from the sale of his parents' house, so he splashed out without telling Sally.

Sam followed CNN all day when Sally was at work. He didn't need to work – not now he had the money. He'd given up his job at the bookshop the day the cheque came through from the solicitor. He liked to watch reports late into the night. Live from Sarajevo. The Market Square Massacre. That's what the banner in the top left corner of the screen said – accompanied by images of twisted metal, charred wood and streaks of blood on punctured concrete. Sam felt enormously moved by these scenes. Moved to tears at men, women and children standing among the devastation.

And he felt excited. After the market square, pressure was on NATO to go in and bomb the Serbs, lying in their dirty little fox holes in the dark ring of mountains that besieged Sarajevo. A can of beer in one hand, the remote in the other, Sam would shout at the generals and politicians. Go on, he'd yell, bomb them to fucking oblivion.

The phone rang. Sally answered. 'It's your sister,' she said.

'Say hi from me,' Sam said, turning the sound up on the television.

'She wants to know if you want to go to the garden of rest – it's your mum's birthday.'

'Tell her I'm busy,' he said. 'I don't feel well.'

Sometimes it was all US economics and manufacturing on CNN. Meaningless. But he was happy to wait for a story to grip him. For breaking news. Something barbaric. Rwanda was quiet now. It had been a flash in the pan. And genocide wasn't quite the same when it was in Africa. Sarajevo had been going on for so long it had dropped off the main bulletins. Sam wanted something new. Another attack on Iraq. A Falklands invasion. Something he could wring his hands over. Something to take his mind off his sister's calls and Sally's questions and the fact that his parents were dead and everyone was always going on about it. It was a fact. They were dead. Full stop. Why couldn't they get over it? What he really needed was a Spanish Civil War. A Holocaust. A comet speeding towards earth, with the chance that they'd all be smashed to pieces as they sat monitoring it on their TV screens. So he drank and waited, watching trivial news stories repeated every thirty minutes, holding out for snippets from Bosnia, wishing he could go out there to see what was really happening, to help the people he saw bent double on his screen every night.

Sally came home all purposeful one evening. She had a bottle of wine. 'Will you turn the TV off?' she said. 'I want to talk to you.'

There was nothing on the news, except transport and health, so he turned it off and took a glass from her.

'I'm worried about you,' she said.

'Don't be,' he said.

'Your mum died a year ago today,' she said.

'Really?' he said, although he knew.

'And you have to start to grieve,' she said. 'For her and your dad.'

This again! he thought. He felt angry, but he would not snap at her. He would be calm. 'I have grieved,' he said. 'At the funerals, remember?'

'You've shown more grief for the people of Bosnia than you have for your parents,' she said.

Why couldn't they realise that compared to Bosnia, their own problems were nothing? 'Don't you know what's going on over there?' he said.

'More than I do what's going on in your head,' she said.

'It's like the Holocaust' he said. 'But it's happening now.'

'I want to talk about *you*,' she said.

'What about me? I don't matter.' He pointed at the blank screen. 'These people matter.'

She lost her temper. 'Well why don't you just go over there and help them then, instead of getting off on watching them suffer on TV?'

'You think I'm getting off on it?'

'I'm worried about you.'

'You think I'm getting off on it?' His voice was louder.

'No,' Sally said. 'I'm just worried about you.'

'Maybe I will go out there,' he said.

'Don't be stupid.'

'It'd be stupid?' he said. 'You think it'd be stupid?'

'Yes,' she said. 'It would be stupid.'

'I'll go,' he said. 'I'll go and help.'

'Help? What can you do to help *them*?'

'Whatever they want me to do.'

'I think you should deal with your problems here before you start on the Balkans,' Sally said.

'What problems do I have here?'

'Sam!'

Sam felt his skin prickle. He was furious at her tone of voice. 'I'm going,' he said.

'You're not, Sam,' she said.

There it was again. She was using his name in *that* tone of voice, treating him like a little boy, a little boy who didn't know his own mind.

'Fuck it,' he said. 'I'm going.'

The ship pulled out into the blackest of seas. With no light from the moon, the Italian coast was swallowed up quickly by the night. At first it was exhilarating. To be out there in the middle of nothing, the wind coming in bursts, the reek of burned fuel filling his lungs. It was as if the break-up with Sally and the death of his parents didn't really matter. But, staring down at the waves, it occurred to him how easy it would be to leap over the railings. One or two seconds of falling through the cold air, then hitting the surface and going under. And he wouldn't even need to leap. Just a slight adjustment of the weight of his body and he would be in the sea.

Dozing for a few hours in the bar, he couldn't get rid of the idea of floating in the water, the light from the ship disappearing, his body giving in.

He woke at 6 a.m., surprised that the mountains of Bosnia were already in view. They were huge. Like a towering cloud bank. He looked deep into the clefts between mountains as the light from the sun defined them. He imagined valleys, chasms and endless forests. He knew that some of the peaks he could see would be casting shadows over Sarajevo. And the thought thrilled him.

At the Dubrovnik ferry terminal Sam sat down in a bar and watched. These were real Yugoslavs – people who had been touched by war. He felt excited and terrified at the same time. And envious. A man came past: thick set, a heavy stubble, a glint in his eye. A young woman, her face half-covered by a scarf. An older man with a crutch, placing a foot carefully as he stepped down from a kerb. A murderer. A rape camp survivor. A landmine victim. He knew these people. He had seen them all on CNN a hundred times.

He found a cheap hotel and dumped his bags. After the port, he wanted to see what the real Dubrovnik was like – the old town. It was there that he hoped to hook up with someone. Someone who could get him into Bosnia. He'd not hang around here for long. This was not a holiday. He was here to do something. Something good.

Sam walked the streets of the old town. It was magnificent. Churches, monasteries, gardens, shops and bars all melded together on a beautiful outcrop of rock, surrounded by a twenty foot thick wall. He found a bar on one of the tight black alleys off the main street and immediately homed in on a couple talking in English at the next table. For an hour he sat listening to them, drinking to calm his nerves, his head full of questions about what the hell he was doing in the Balkans. Plucking up courage – drunk – he went over to their table.

'I've just got here today,' he said. 'Can I join you?'

Lloyd was a journalist. And English. The woman was from near Sarajevo.

'I am Jasmina,' she said, grinning

Sam couldn't take his eyes off her long brown hair and a low cut top showing her cleavage. And she stared right into his eyes when he talked to her. Lloyd was quiet, watching him, but he seemed friendly enough. They asked him why he was in Dubrovnik and he explained.

'I might be able to help,' Lloyd said. 'I've a mate who does aid runs – convoys – into Bosnia. One tomorrow. From here.' But it was dangerous, he said. On the trip before last, one of the drivers had been shot.

Sam felt good. Here he was in the Balkans, with someone who could help him get involved, with a woman who was giving him the eye. All on his first night. He wished Sally could see him now.

Eventually Lloyd left, saying Sam should come to the north gate of the old town, by the bus terminus, at 7 a.m. the next day, to see if he was okay for the trip.

Jasmina stayed. Sam bought her drinks for a couple of hours and she sat with him, laughing, touching his thigh, rolling her eyes upwards so he could stare at her body. Late in the evening, both of them drunk, she asked him why he was really going to Bosnia.

'No one wants to go into there,' she said. 'Only fools.'

'I needed to get away,' he said.

'From who?'

'My life,' he said, aware he must sound pathetic to anyone from Sarajevo.

She waved away his apologies. 'And a woman?' she said.

'Yes,' he said, smiling.

'Is that all?' she said, smiling too.

Then he surprised himself. 'My mother died,' he said. 'A year or so ago. And my dad. A couple of years before that.'

She nodded, paused, and asked 'How did they die?'

'Cancer. Both of them.'

'Do you miss them?' she said.

He was shocked by her question. 'I don't know,' he said. 'I've not thought about it.'

'You don't think about it every day?'

·'Never,' he said. Then: 'What about your parents? Are they here?'

'They are dead,' she said.

'I'm sorry,' he said.

'It is the same story as you. Your parents are dead. My parents are dead.'

He paid her after he slept with her. The equivalent of eight pounds. He came away from her flat feeling euphoric. He had slept with a prostitute. Was she a prostitute? She had slept with him for money. But it had been more than that, he thought. They had connected. He had said things to her that he had not even thought before. And she had asked to see him the next night. He said he would be in Bosnia by then.

She smiled and said 'Well, if you are…'

A few hours later – at 6.30 a.m. – Sam had checked out of his hotel and found a place on the city wall to wait for the convoy. He had not slept. The thought of going into Bosnia terrified him. But he wanted to do what Sally said he would never do. He would go. He would take on his fears and go.

Just after seven, he heard rumbling. From a tunnel to the right, three old trucks that looked like war film cast-offs emerged. Lloyd appeared from the north gate of the old town and waved the trucks down. He looked around impatiently, then at his watch. Sam had come down off the walls and was hidden in the shadow of the north gate. He remained frozen to the spot. He saw Lloyd talking to someone in the front truck, then run to the second truck and get in. Sam couldn't move. The three trucks revved their engines and set off, south on the Split road.

What the fuck had he been thinking? Had he really meant to go into Bosnia past army checkpoints, to be shot at, to find himself in the heart of a war zone? His legs felt weak. Sally had been right all along. This was as far as he would get.

Sam walked round the wall to look at the sea. The Adriatic was surging, water hitting the base of the wall, then being sucked back across the rocks. He looked north along the coast. The trucks were out of Dubrovnik, climbing a hill, three shapes in the distance. He was almost laughing. That he had thought he could go to Bosnia. To be in a war. To be among people he knew nothing about.

He felt exhausted and stared down at the water and was struck by the clearest of memories. Sea fishing with his father. The waves round the bottom of the harbour. The smell of the salt in the sea. His father, arms around him, showing him how to hold the rod, how to work the reel. The memory caught him off guard. And he was crying, slumped on the cold stone of the wall. This was not a little moisture he could wipe away, but a sobbing, leaving him breathless, tears streaming down his face, not caring who could see him or hear him, and underneath it all, there was an elation, a feeling that he was not actually crying, but laughing. Because *this* was the first nice memory he had had of his parents, the first memory that was not about coughed up blood and the smell of a room where two people had died.

'When you were young?'

After a few drinks, they were at Jasmina's flat again.

'When I was young?' she said, pulling a face. 'What do you mean?'

'Did your parents die when you were young?'

'No,' she said. 'Two years ago.'

People always thought Sam's parents had died in a car accident. Because they had died close together. But he knew Jasmina's parents had not died in a car accident. He had been there an hour. He didn't want sex. She knew that. She smiled as he waited for her to speak.

'They were murdered,' she said.

He didn't know what to say. 'I'm sorry,' he said eventually.

She was watching him. 'When the paramilitaries came it was morning,' she said. 'They took all the men. We knew they might kill them. But my mother did nothing. She just touched my father's hand when he walked towards the soldiers. He made with his eyes that I should stand at the back, behind the older women. That was the last thing – then he was gone. Into a bus. Like he was going away to work. Then they came to take all the women. But not the old women.' Jasmina looked out of the window. 'And my mother went forward, but they signalled that I should go forward. You could smell the alcohol on their breath. The soldiers. They were wired. Is that what you say? And my mother went forward again, pushing me back. But a soldier came and led me out. So my mother jumped on him, pulling his hair. And he laughed and pushed her over. Then he shot her,' she said. And not stopping 'I have two brothers. Boys. In Sarajevo. I have a friend who can get them out for $2000. That is why I am in Dubrovnik.' And then she said nothing. She didn't fill in any of the gaps in her story. She just stared at the tapestry on the wall.

'I'm stupid,' Sam said, standing up. 'I told you about my parents. And it's trivial. After what you have been through. I'm sorry.'

'You *are* stupid,' she said. 'If you think that.'

Sam walked through the old town. It was 2 a.m. Finding a gap in the walls, he went to the pier, a hundred yards of stone jutting out from the harbour. The wind was coming off the sea, rushing inland like the air being drawn into a fire grate. He felt ridiculous. What was he doing here? Still here? It was absurd. Why had he come a thousand miles to grieve people who had died at home? He could do nothing in Bosnia. Nothing good. He had never actually defined anything good he could do. It had been a stupid fantasy. He was insulting the people here, people he really knew nothing about. The only good thing he could do was leave. He felt for his wallet in his pocket. His tickets home. His passport. His money...

He walked up the steps to Jasmina's flat with a Thomas Cook envelope containing six hundred pounds. He dropped it through the letterbox and went quickly down the stairs. At the port he found a phone and called Sally.

About a Boy, a Man and a Duck

Philip Hughes

James likes to feed the ducks and sometimes he doesn't eat most of his sandwiches so he can feed them after school. His favourite duck is Henry The Duck. He looks like he has a little green moustache and is always most grateful when James shares out his lunch.

Henry The Duck (the duck) was a duck and had been all his life. He started off as a little duck egg, then he hatched into a little duck, then he grew into a small duck then he ate and ate and ate till he became a BIG duck. He was the biggest, fastest duck on any pond in any park anywhere in the Midlands. Most of the other ducks were mean to Henry The Duck (the duck). They were jealous of his big beak, his big feathers and his cracking sense of humour. He would have all the lady ducks fluttering their eyelashes at him or wiggling their little duck tails in his direction. It is a myth that lady ducks prefer a sense of humour to looks and muscles but, having all three, Henry The Duck (the duck) was flavour of the month every month and most of the nests around the park that year would be producing lots of little Henry The Ducks – and Henriettas.

Henry The Duck's best friend in the whole of the Midlands was not another duck or even Uncle Dave The Pike (who was not really an uncle, just a close friend of the family). No Henry The Duck's best friend was James, a seven-year-old boy from a broken home on the estate.

James walks the long way back to the flat through the park to see Henry The Duck every day, even if he has no sandwiches to share, and Henry The Duck will drop whatever important duck business he is tending to as soon as he spies James at the park gates.

At the park a man always asks James if he wants a Jelly Baby and James likes Jelly Babies especially the green ones, but the man always holds the bag too tight and he can't ever get one out.

Henry The Duck doesn't trust many people, and he certainly doesn't trust the old man who stands quietly by the side of the pond eating Jelly Babies from the pocket of an old parka.

He has more at his house, but Henry The Duck knows that trick.

It unnerves him the way the man salivates when James arrives, unnerves him the way he shuffles closer and closer and closer to James before offering him a Jelly Baby.

He has more at his house.

Henry The Duck isn't sure James knows that trick.

Today James gets his whole hand in the packet and is dismayed to find it empty. The dirty old man has tricked him. And the man smells.

He has more at his house. James picks the wrapper out of the lake so no ducks will get hurt. He'd prefer not to go home. Dad would be home and he never has sweets, only bad moods and worse tempers. It wouldn't be far either and Henry The Duck would come along to look after him. Henry The Duck was his best friend in the whole of the Midlands. Most boys his age were only interested in smashing cars or killing stuff, but not James. Henry The Duck understood him. Henry The Duck looked after him. Sometimes when it was dark and the shouting in the flat was so loud no-one slept, James would sneak out with his clothes over his pyjamas and go to see Henry The Duck. Henry The Duck would be sitting on another duck chatting but then would fly over as soon as he saw James.

Henry The Duck ruffles his feathers as James's hand gets stuck in the yellow packet and finally wriggles out empty. The packet falls lightly into the water. *He has more at his house.*

James doesn't know that trick.

Henry The Duck follows as man and small boy walk away from the park, away from the estate.

Henry The Duck follows to look after his best friend James.

Henry The Duck followed James and James followed the dirty old man. The dirty old man kept checking to see if James was following. James was following. The man really, really smelt.

Simon is a dirty old man in many senses of the word – he both doesn't wash and he steals women's panties from laundrettes. He also likes Jelly

Babies especially the green ones. He always offers sweets to be polite but gets anxious when people linger over their selection. He would like to feed the ducks but never has sandwiches for lunch to not eat and so can't feed the ducks. Instead he stands and watches a young boy waste corned beef amongst the floating syringes and shopping trolleys. Simon was hungry and although he didn't trust the boy – the boy looked like he liked jelly babies almost as much as he did – the boy had a duck. Simon was hungry but it was only polite to offer. To his embarrassment, however, the packet was empty; he dropped it in the pond and offered to get some more from his house. The boy agreed. It would be OK; he would remove all the green ones before the boy got his hands to them.

The duck follows the trail of bread and corned beef James drops behind him. He doesn't miss a single one. Man and small boy walk on, away from the park, away from the estate.

Simon was hungry. The duck followed.

The dirty old man led the small boy back to the house. The small boy followed the dirty old man. Henry The Duck followed the small boy.

One cannot survive on Jelly Babies alone.

James ate a red jelly baby.

Simon ate Henry The Duck.

James walked home alone.

When Silence is the Only Thing we Leave Behind

Maria Roberts

It's ten o'clock Sunday evening when my mother calls. I am drinking white wine from a mug. Pilar is next to me chatting into her mobile to Sasha her Russian boyfriend. I suspect that they are talking about me. I suspect that I am being paranoid. Since she arrived a week ago, I have been as moody as sin. Yesterday afternoon I stormed into the room and bellowed at her because the television was too loud. I made her cry. She irritates the hell out of me. I am messy, worse than usual, and she has spent this past week clearing away my dishes, moving scraps of paper from surface to surface and hoovering up biscuit crumbs, dried egg and crisps from the floor. I have many other faults; like chewing gum all day and twiddling my little finger in my mouth. What drives me mad about Pilar is that she cuts her toenails in the living room – that and her unwillingness to speak English on the phone.

I imagine she is telling Sasha what a poor host I am; that she hates it here and wishes she could go back home. I have not taken her out once. It has rained every day.

I have allowed Pilar to have the run of the place. When I arrive home from work I find her slouched at my desk tapping away on chat sites or using my hairdryer to scrunch bigger curls into her hair. I have no privacy. She sees everything about me. In my room there are glasses scattered on top of furniture with little pools of red wine congealing like wounds inside. There are ashtrays too; in the kitchen, by the bed, on the bookcase. The truth is I don't usually smoke. Her presence here is making me feel embarrassed and exposed. Already I want her to go.

It is as though I have obtained an overgrown child. Pilar is foolish and skittish. Her energy like her wild curly hair fills too much space in this small room. On early mornings when she dashes from her bed to the shower, she blocks out the sun. Now she clicks the stem of the wine glass. Her thin fingers and long nails are like the claws of a bird.

I twitch uncomfortably and stare at her hard. She winks at me, pulls her legs up and tucks her chin into her knees. She leans into the phone.

They talk a mixture of Catalan and Russian but not Spanish. She twiddles with a ring on her little toe, pushing it round and round, round and round. She straightens a curl tight and it twangs back. She wraps a coil around a finger then watches it bounce in that small space between her eyes. I sense that she is in love. I despise how she coos to him.

My mother has been talking for some time. Ten minutes perhaps. There isn't a clock in the house so it is hard to tell. She says, 'so tomorrow at two o'clock. Do you want me to come with you?'

By the way she coughs I can tell that she expects a reply.

'No thank you.'

'Is everything okay there?' This is a foolish question, I think, given the circumstances.

My mother sighs so I oblige and say, 'Yes, it's all fine.'

'If you want me to come with you, just call me and I will.' A clever response when she knows that I won't.

'I'll want to talk to him, mother.' And then for clarity add, 'on my own.'

My family consider solitude strange; they cohort in groups or packs. They shop in fours and sleep in twos. We holiday in fives: father, mother, sister, her husband and lonely ole me.

My mother sounds sleepy. She tells me that she has been cleaning all day and if I'm hungry tomorrow, around lunch time, and want to pop in then to do so because she plans to bake some scones and a couple of apple pies. I could take one home to share with Pilar. I tell her that it is kind but Pilar will not eat pie because she claims to have a wheat intolerance and follows a restricted diet.

I tell her that she is tired and so am I; we can we talk tomorrow. Then I hang up when she is in the middle of saying goodbye.

I go into the kitchen and empty what remains of the wine into my mug. I expect Pilar shouldn't mind. She isn't a great drinker. I have drunk every night for almost three weeks. I spend the mornings vomiting in the bathroom, careful to wipe away what misses the bowl. This morning I woke at five o'clock and vomited intermittently until nine. My throat burned. This evening my kidneys ache my back. I like the emptiness being sick leaves behind. I have not eaten either and so I expect that in a few hours it shall start again. I am slightly tipsy, I'll admit.

Pilar is carefree. I like that about her. She has no interest in current affairs. She has no religion. She knows little about Easter and Christmas. She says this is because she is not affiliated to a church. Her parents are from Iran. They used to be Muslim. Spain is a Catholic country, I told her. Jesus is big over there. Half the nation is called Jesus and the other half is called Maria. How can you not know about Easter? 'I don't,' she said and then continued to massage strengthening oil into her toenails. Later with some tweezers she picked out wiry hairs.

It is difficult to talk to Pilar about things. She has stayed with me for a month, every year, for the past four years. We met at University but I can't say that we were ever really friends. We were language exchange students: her English was perfect even then and my Spanish, like now, was very poor. When I picked her up from the airport last Sunday she informed me that I have put on too much weight and she does not like the colour I have dyed my hair. From experience I have learned that when it comes to Pilar, the best form of defence is simply not to reply.

Pilar's teeth are very white and her skin is toffee brown. Her father is a dentist, her mother is a chiropractor and her elder brother is studying for a PhD in Biochemistry. Her boyfriend teaches Physics at Bangor University (but she will not go to visit him because she thinks that Wales is too far, and too cold). It baffles me that she can be surrounded by such intellectuals when her only interest is which product will limit the frizz of her hair or which lipstick she should wear. Covering my stacks of unopened letters and random scribbled notes are her piles of glossy magazines. When she is cooking some odd concoction combining couscous and tomatoes, I flick through the fashion pages. Sometimes I almost enjoy her being here.

We have come to an agreement that I should leave notes on the stairs when I do not wish to be disturbed. This worked for a day but as my writing is barely legible, she would knock on my bedroom door and wave the paper wildly above her head, ranting that she cannot read such scrawling. When I tell her that the notes say *Do Not Knock On My Door* she laughs hysterically then sits down on the bed and tells me everything that Sasha has done that day. She prints off his emails and shows me these too. Only yesterday she presented me with his clearance letter from the

G.U.M. clinic.

I like to read but she says that reading is boring. She cannot stand books; who on earth would want to read a book for fun? I'm not sure. All of the books I read make me cry. She said, 'Do you like to cry?' I thought for a moment and came to the conclusion that I suppose, yes, I do. The thing is I haven't cried yet. When Sue called to tell me what had happened, I thanked her and then said goodbye.

I'd like to go into the living room and watch TV but she is kicking her legs out with each fit of giggles and then tucking them back in under her bottom. I wonder if she and Sasha have ever had phone sex. They have a long distant relationship and she has spent much of her time talking to him with her head on the pillow and a hand between her legs.

She is a virgin. I think this because she asks too many questions about sex. Pilar thinks that I am an expert when it comes to coital matters because I am a divorcee. What do men like? She probes. I'm quick to point out that I am probably not the best person to ask. I married at eighteen and he left six months later. I have not seen Peter since, and in the past eight years I have had sex only five times and with two different men. The last time a man came near my door it was to sell life insurance and like a fool I sent him away. My advice, I told her, is to do everything to begin with and then manipulate it back triple fold. My aphorism on love is that each relationship should be entered into as though it were a competition: peak early on and it could spell disaster; go too slow and you're out of the race; cheat and you lose self respect. And finally: always, always, keep your hands on his balls. On hearing this Pilar tutted, shook her head and told me to seek help. Like I said, I'm probably not the best person to ask for advice. I'm bitter before I'm old. Peter, by the way, left me for the navy. When we first met he said he was a pacifist. Turns out he lied.

My mother says it turned out he lied about almost everything. Sue, Peter's mother, lives two roads away from my grandma. His grandma and my grandma were friends from church. I met Peter the day of his grandfather's funeral. He wore desert boots and Joe Bloggs 21 inch flares that had been passed down to him by his elder brother. I thought he looked ridiculous and told him. He said he thought I looked cute and asked if I wanted to catch *The Exorcist* at the cinema in Salford. We caught a taxi there and walked back hand in hand. I didn't even like horror movies. Every time I ducked under his arm or covered my eyes, he laughed. He was sweet then with his scrawny purple mottled limbs and a hollow pit under his ribcage that could hold a golf ball. It was a good party trick. I was portly in contrast but he didn't seem to mind. My mother called him Jack. Three months after we met he proposed. We picked the ring from the Argos catalogue. Two months later we moved into a bedsit above Dillon's newsagents in Davyhulme. They gave us a discount on the rent and as a favour I helped Mr Snape put the Sunday supplements in the papers. Within the year I'd had the abortion.

I tell Pilar that she shouldn't give in so freely to Sasha. He calls too often and that worries me. He sends flowers, expensive gifts and love notes sprayed in aftershave. Last year she had been here just three days when Parcel Force handed over a small box containing a swish looking digital camera. He says he wants to marry her. To him she says that she is too young but to me she admits that it is because his mother is a pig farmer and her family would not approve.

I wondered about Peter a lot. There were other loves in my life. Brief flings, you know; the kind that last about a month but kill you with their overwhelming intensity. Every man I meet I want to marry. I'm a walking cliché. Peter was a love: fair hair that fell clumsily over his eyes, small ears, blue eyes that turned grey on cold days, and a rash on his chin. I lost my virginity on the top of a double-decker night bus. We were on our way home from a big night out in town. It was in the days before CCTV when all the surveillance the buses had was a cleverly positioned mirror. You could smoke on buses then. I remember because afterwards we shared a fag we'd found stuck down the side of the seat. He wrote I Love You in lipstick on the ceiling and I drew a great big heart in the dirt on the window.

Funny, isn't it, how when all your memories are stripped away only the good ones remain. We are sitting on a bench beneath the kitchen window at my mother's, she's hung hanging baskets everywhere and marigolds are taking over the world. There's a pot beside us with a great blooming red geranium. We're sipping shandy. 'On a Ragga Tip' is on the radio next door, there is a dog barking, and a butterfly playing in the firs. We're talking about where we plan to go that night. I can't remember where we decided. I'm sitting here on my bed, feet up, hands behind my head, and I swear to you, I cannot remember one single word. I want to. It's never bothered me before. It's bugging me now. Where did we say we'd go? I think I need some more wine.

Wine solves nothing. I found the remains of an old bottle of pudding wine at the back of the cupboard and I have spent the past half hour being sick. Pilar made a whinnying sound like a horse being buggered. She didn't come to check that I am OK she just snorted 'Saaaaaally you okaaay?' No I'm fucking not okay. That's plain to see. She's still chunnering away on the phone. She hasn't moved for over an hour.

Is the room covered in a magical mist or are my eyes watering? I don't give a fuck. In the morning Pilar will say, 'Did you drink all that wine?' (I wouldn't leave it now would I? You have to be quick in this house.) 'Why?' (Because I like getting wasted and it ends the day well.) 'Don't you feel sick?' (I'll lie 'No, not at all' when the truth is: 'Of course I fucking do.') I don't think she'll come to visit again. I don't think I care.

Let me think about Peter.

A few days after our first date he turned up outside the yard, red bomber jacket, blue jeans, and a red moped. I heard him coming then lay on my belly on the kitchen floor. I heard him bound up the steps and knock on the back door. We laughed about it months after; he said he had known that I was lying face down on the lino and that was why he had waited so long on the step. I explained that I was shy and scared; most of my friends had lost their virginity by then; I had only just had my first kiss.

She is still cackling; I'm going to have to shut my bedroom door. I tell you there is nothing worse than someone else's happiness when you are feeling worse than shite. It makes you want to drive a stake through their heart.

Peter was always in trouble. He was arrested at twelve for cow tipping, thirteen for graffiti and fifteen for nicking his mother's car. I was attracted to the sense of adventure that pulsated within him. Now I'm older I can see that what I was attracted to was the excitement that pulsated in his pants.

He had life, you know, loads of it. Some people go through life looking like a washed-up carcass. Too like their parents or soulless. I hate soulless people. Pilar's soul is as shallow as a puddle. Not that she cares. She cares about fuck all that one. Peter's soul was full. He had a quirkiness about him. He had happiness. He swaggered. You could beat him with a stick, throw shit in his face and those blue eyes would peak through those curls, his cheeks would puff out with a grin and then he'd be gone; the drone of his moped resonating in the alleyway. My mother disapproved, of course, (when doesn't she?) but when you are young, and when you are in love then nothing matters. Not your mates or your job or college, nothing.

Why do people tell lies? That's what I want to know. There are other important questions pressing through my mind right now, like why do I never buy enough wine? Why can't wine be delivered on mountain bikes like amphetamines? Some of us have drink problems (but live in constant denial, for example buying just one bottle at the supermarket when we actually need two). The last of the summer wine has gone. I've been on white wine this evening and now a small pool is sitting at the bottom of the mug like a poor piss sample. I should drink my piss; last time I tried it was a middle of the range medium dry.

I am bothered. What vestige should one wear when visiting the dead? Black seems wrong. Peter liked me in pale blue: the only pale blue I have is an old angora jumper my mum bought me for my sixteenth birthday. He liked it. If I can fit into that sweater then that is what I shall wear. Jeans or trousers? Probably jeans. Sue said the last time she spoke to him he asked about me. There was no girlfriend or wife or kids like I imagined. He said, 'Mum I wish things had been different with me and Sally.' She said, 'Yeah, I know.'

I am at Tolton and Sons. Anybody born in Stretford will end up sucking eggs here a few days before the soil is shoved over them or they are pushed into the incinerator. The waiting room is too nice. Print flowered wallpaper, appliquéd curtains, flower printed carpet. I've been reading the coffin price list. I wonder if Sue will go for the dear do or the cheap one. We're burning him anyway. I'd be sensible and opt for the cheapest. Sue probably won't. And then there is the cost of the cars, £100 an hour. We should take him there ourselves and donate the money to charity. He was brought back to Manchester from Weston-Super-Mare at a cost of over £1 a mile here and the same back. 'He had to be kept cool,' she said. 'We would have done it ourselves otherwise.' I'm going to try not to cry, but there are tissues there on the coffee table next to a prayer card. They expect you to cry here. I can't guarantee I will, I can't guarantee I won't. He's been dead three weeks now and I have to keep reminding myself that he's gone. I think of those felt tips my friend Paula had when we were fifteen. You cover the page in colour then sweep the magic pen over in any squirly fashion you like. I usually drew hearts or cats. The black turned pink, the green turned yellow, the yellow turned invisible. Peter is invisible now. I'm trying hard to remember little details like how he laughed, what food he liked, the brand of beer, whether he wanted brown or red sauce on his bacon butties on a Sunday morning. All I know is that he took three sugars in his tea. It doesn't even taste like tea when you put that many sugars in. I'd say, 'you'll rot your teeth.' He'd say, 'Woman, leave me be and let me drink my tea.'

'You must be Mrs Wood.' The man at the door looks as fusty as a stuffed penguin. He bows his head at me. He stands reverently, hands and arms crossed at the hip, swinging softly. Like a footballer, only we're not here to play ball. He's making me feel nervous. I sense that he wants me to lower my head and walk solemnly with him down the hall. I hold my head up high and look around. We are young, I want to say, not old like you. Don't make me behave as though Peter were as old as you. So I smile as best I can.

'Yes. My name is Sally.' It is a rather stupid reply but it's all I could manage. He nods reassuringly at me. I add, 'It's very rainy outside, isn't it?'

There isn't any music looping in the background and he leads me from the waiting room down a magnolia hall. There are piles of flowers by the door waiting for a car. White carnations spell out the word Nana. When we get to the end I see that Nana is Ethel Walker D.o.b. 01.12.1927. I make the sign of the cross and think for a moment. Nana. She'll be sorely missed. The director looks at his feet, then very gently he shifts his gaze to me, 'You know, Mrs Wood, not to touch the body. You are aware that Peter has hepatitis C.' I nod, and sniffle a little. 'Please, Mrs Wood, when you are ready, go in. In your own time.' When he steps to the side I see the brass plate: Peter Wood D.o.b. 17.08.77. Before I can stop myself I begin to cry.

'Shall I take those flowers?'

I've been carrying white roses. More appropriate for a man and I think Peter would like them. The edges of the petals are turning brown. They don't look as good as they did an hour ago. I shake my head.

'No thanks. I'll take them in.'

He pats my arm, bows and then leaves. I have never seen a dead person before. I'm not sure what to expect. I hear Mr Tolton pad along the carpet. I see that he is bow legged. He rubs his moustache, his posture is stooped, but his shoulders poke up as though a hanger is stuffed down his back. I pity him. It must be a challenge to deal with the dead and the morose. I suspect it would put you off life.

Does he know the circumstances of Peter's death? Probably. He orchestrated the make-up and told Sue they would do what they could to patch up the scars. I'm feeling sick standing here. Perhaps I won't go in after all. Nothing to see, move along, move along. Move along in. That's what I should do. I can hear the clacking of the ventilation. I've taken a few days off work. The funeral is tomorrow. I told Margaret at the Agency that I was taking a last minute mid-week break. I wasn't quite sure what to say. If I told the truth they would ask how he died. I can't say the truth. Peter was found in a public toilet near Winter Gardens with a needle jutting out from his damaged veins. I think of those last moments and all I can imagine is that he was so very alone. I never got round to changing my name. I don't remember which year we filed for divorce. There were nights when I imagined he was out at sea wishing he was still mine.

He was found early Sunday morning. Usual story: Man Out Walking Dog Finds Body. It made the news. An unidentified male age 26-34 was yesterday found dead in a public toilet. Rogue batch of heroin. The second in as many weeks. Lethal. It was five days before the police located Sue.

I suppose I'm scared. I want Peter to look safe.

A simple wedding at Gretna Green. We'd seen it in a soap opera and followed suit. I bought my dress from a posh charity shop in Altrincham. We bought some champagne at a late shop and took it back to the B&B. We made love all night. We took photos with a disposable camera. We lost the camera.

The door is lighter than I imagined it would be. There's little force, just a soft swoosh. The emptiness is overwhelming. I stand for a moment. I look out of the window. I know that when I look at him he will have changed.

Peter is yellow grey, his hands are purple, there are wounds on his knuckles, his face is hollow but puffed out as though they've pushed two Victoria plums in there. His eyes are closed, he has too much stubble, his lips are hard. Beneath the shroud I see that he is naked. He looks old.

When I say hello, he doesn't reply, but then he could be a quiet man when it took his fancy. He was broody that night he left.

When the police called to Sue's and told her to sit down, she knew that it was bad news but cracked on with the jokes anyway. She expected to be presented with a box of his belongings but when she put this to the officer she was told he didn't have any possessions. Peter didn't have a home. There was nothing to send back to us. She asked me if I'd kept anything and I had to admit that everything he left behind that day I took to the tip or the charity shop. I shredded the photos. I even changed the furniture. Of Peter's life we have nothing. Not one thing. He listened to the Eagles, the Beach Boys and U2. His favourite song, says Sue, was *Desperado*. I'd always thought it was *Hotel California*. It's a small thing, but I want to know. She said that they will play *Desperado* at the funeral. I asked her if he had any friends. She said she doesn't know, but she didn't think so. Did I remember any names from his school days? Michael, I offer, but it draws a blank and we agree that it should be a small affair with catering at the Nag's Head for about twenty people.

I want to know where he has been and why in all those years he never came home. I tell him that I missed him and despite everything we all loved him. I tell him we are sorry we let him down but he can be happy now. Whatever pain there was has gone.

The silence seems to last forever.

I pull up a chair close to him; behind his left ear I see faint purple pin marks. I tried to imagine the man he had become but I can only see the boy that I knew. Then I close my eyes and sing to him.

Oh Desperado, why don't you come to your senses?

For a moment I can feel him near me.

These things that are pleasing you can hurt you somehow.

His hands are large and warm.

Now it seems to me some fine things have been laid upon your table but you only want the ones that you can't get.

I'm trying to remember the tunes he hummed and I wonder if I'm singing out of time. We sat together in the bath, washing one another, listening to this album over and over again.

My voice is shaking a little; it is difficult to capture the right tone. It's getting to the hard bit. I practised this at home for months after he'd gone in case he called.

It may be raining but there's a rainbow above you.

My head hurts with the strain and my chest feels hot but I can hear his whispers in the wind. I am listening for his voice and when it comes it is smooth against my ears.

You better let somebody love you.

He is beside me; his breath soft against my hair.

You better let somebody love you.

His arm is around my waist

You better let somebody love you, before it's too late.

He is holding me tight now but the grief and the loss, it hurts my insides.

The Last Day

Rory Miller

It was the last day and we wanted to sleep in, but Jonathan came in early complaining about a toothache. He was in pain, all right, but what could I do? He sat on the bed and whimpered while Meg stuck her fingers in his mouth and peered inside. She had her concerned face on. I said, how about some whisky? Meg looked at me. She said, you can't give a three-year-old whisky. She turned back to Jonathan and then went into the bathroom. I heard her open the cabinet door and move things around. I said, what difference does it make? Jonathan looked at me. It went quiet. She came back in with her toothbrush in her hand. I can't find anything, she said. I took that as a green light. I got up and fetched the whisky and two glasses and poured us boys a drink.

Last night Meg and I had tried to get down to it – to go out in style, you know – but it wasn't happening. I felt so crazy inside. I said, just hold me. She put her arms around me and I cried into her hair. She said, don't cry, Don, it'll be all right. She rubbed my back and kissed my face, and then she talked about where she wanted to be born next. There's other planets, Don, she said, more life to live. She really believed that. She said, I'd like to be with you again, if you want to. She said, maybe I could be the man next time, and we laughed. I felt so close to her. I held her tight and then I went under the covers and inhaled every little part of her. Her skin was exquisite. She said, what are you doing? I said, just let me smell you.

I got up a few hours later and walked downstairs in my boxers. I unplugged the TV and carried it down to the basement. Then I thought, what the hell. I took it out into the yard and laid into it with my hammer. The screen was gone in a second. I felt a piece of glass catch me on the cheek and I put my finger to where it hit. It was bleeding. I sucked the finger and then carried on with my hammering. Meg came down and stood on the porch. She looked sleepy. I smiled at her and said, want a go? She wiped her eyes and said, come to bed. I looked at the TV and then put the hammer in the back of the truck. I took her hand and followed her upstairs.

We ate breakfast and then she went with Jonathan to get washed up. I went out to the yard to hide the wrecked TV. I didn't want him seeing it. I looked up and saw the sun over the trees and reckoned we had about fourteen hours. Hopefully we'd be sleeping by then. Hopefully we'd be out of it and wouldn't feel a thing. I knew others wouldn't be so lucky. In some places it would be the middle of the day. In some places it would be tidal waves and clouds of dust, and no one knew how long that would take. We were less than a thousand miles from where it was supposed to hit and they'd told us it would be pretty instantaneous. I hoped so. It was bad enough as it was.

I cleared away the breakfast things and washed the dishes. Meg came in the room and asked me, what did I want to do today? She was smiling and holding a bunch of wild flowers. She gave them to me. She kissed me on the cheek and said, I love you. I took her in my arms. I said, I can't think of a damn thing. She leaned back and looked at me. Let's go to the pond, she said. She turned her head and called Jonathan. He came in clutching a video.

We shared the pond with three neighbours, couples like Meg and I. We'd all got together about seven years back and bought a chunk of land so we could build our own houses. The pond sat right in the middle of it. Back then we'd meet there to cook up some food and take a swim, etcetera. We were like hippies, I suppose. That was before jobs and kids had taken over.

The others had split nearly a month ago. I guess they wanted to be with their families. When I was sure they weren't coming back, I'd gone over to their places and taken the food, some books, and Steve's golf clubs and balls. I'd hit the balls over the fields and then I'd used the clubs to whale on dad's old truck. He didn't need it anymore and now the clubs were all broken and bent. We hadn't spoken in years.

The last we'd seen of anyone was two weeks back, when we were over at the Johnson's farm. They'd let us come and take what we wanted, and we'd loaded up on apples and pumpkins. That's what we'd been living on – that, and whatever cans had accumulated in the cupboard. Meg had worked wonders with them. She'd been so strong.

Some days it was so nice, when the sun shone and we sat out back, me chopping wood and her trying to conjure up another pumpkin surprise. She'd say to me, what do you want? I'd say, have we got any pumpkin? We cooked over an open fire and drank water from a stream and said how we should have done it more often, how things taste better this way. I'd look at her and wonder where the arguments and bad times had come from, why it hadn't always been like this. We talked so gently to each other. We listened.

Other days I'd say, I wish we were in the city. Meg would look at me like I was crazy. Sure, we'd seen it on TV, before the electricity had gone down, the looting and the violence. I knew it was bad. But out here it was so peaceful I would forget all that. It was like everything was the same. At least in the city I would know what was going on.

But she loved it here. She would wake up and head outside, even when it rained. I'd see her walking barefoot in the grass smelling things, or looking over the fields for hours. She seemed happy. She seemed happier than she ever had. It made me angry sometimes. One time I shouted and told her, don't you know what's happening here? Don't you care? Look at your son, I'd said. I turned and pointed toward him. He was sitting cross-legged watching his videos and saying, shush, his eyes still on the screen. It broke my heart. He was watching a cartoon and when he laughed I laughed with him. I'm sorry, I said, and she held me, running her hand through my hair.

We walked down to the pond. Jonathan wore his blue rubber boots and skipped ahead of us, stopping every now and then to crouch in the grass and point something out. Then he was gone again. Meg and I walked slowly, hand in hand. The leaves were starting to fall and made a sound under our feet. The sun was gentle and golden. The sky was blue. It was a beautiful day. It's hard to imagine, I said. Meg nodded. I said, I wonder what's happening in the cities, in the rest of the world, what are other people doing? I said, we're lucky to be out here. She pulled me closer and we kissed. Jonathan was talking to something in the bushes.
Meg squeezed my hand and asked me if I'd ever been with anyone. I felt my heart miss a beat. I said, no, I haven't. She squeezed again and said, did you ever want to? Did you ever come close? I looked away from her. I thought about it for a minute. Sure, it had crossed my mind, but I knew what would happen, and that was as far as it went. I said, no, when I met you, I never wanted anyone else. It's true, I said, you've always been

enough for me. More than enough, sometimes, I said, and we laughed. She poked me and made a face. She looked at me and I knew she was waiting for me to ask her back. I knew, too, what the answer would be.

We came through the trees to the pond. Meg stood on a fallen aspen and took some deep breaths. I started walking over to my boat. It looked like an oar was missing but Meg called me before I could check it out. I turned and saw her taking off her shoes. Don, she said, let's go for a swim. I looked at the water. It's freezing, I said. She smiled at me and threw a sock my way. So what? she said. She started to strip off. Meg, I said, and I turned to Jonathan. He had his back to us and was looking down at something. Does it matter? she said. She was down to her bra and starting to unbutton her jeans. She stopped for a moment and looked at me. It was crazy, I know, but he'd never seen us naked. I looked at Jonathan again, trying to make out what he was investigating, and when I turned back she was wading into the water. Her bra and panties were with the rest of her clothes, piled on the trunk of the fallen tree. I sat on the ground and watched her. She walked slowly, ripples spreading out across the pond from where her thighs touched the surface. Her ass was beautiful. When she got up to her waist she turned around and smiled at me. It is freezing, she said. Then she went under.
Jonathan came and sat in my lap. What's mommy doing? he said. She's swimming, I said. She's enjoying herself. She was out in the middle now, shouting out and making a noise. I couldn't tell if it was from the cold or something else. Mommy! he shouted, and she waved. He waved back.

We sat together by that pond and we didn't say a word. We watched her as she swam back and forth, and as she trod water and splashed happily on the surface. We watched her as she dove below, and we waited for her to appear again. She was like a mermaid. She took one last look around, then came back to us and walked up out of the water. She stood by her clothes, brushing the drops from her skin. She was in no hurry to get dressed. We looked at her and she let us.

My eyes met hers and I thought, this woman is more familiar to me than my own right hand. I thought, I can't believe I'm never going to see this again. I so much wanted to watch her grow old, to see her hair turn grey, her shape change, all the things I had heard about my whole life. I wanted to be there with her in ten, twenty, thirty years' time. I remembered how we had met, her smile, the things we had said, and I remembered how she had looked when Jonathan was growing inside her. We'd been through so much together. I was sitting there, looking up at her, and I could have worshipped her. I thought, why haven't I felt this always?

Meg shivered all the way home. I gave her my coat and carried her shoes, and when we got in she asked me to make a fire. She brought some blankets and sat next to me while I started it up. Her teeth chattered in my ear and she was laughing. She said she could piss ice-cubes. Jonathan sat in front of her staring at the first flickering flames. Her arms were around him. When the fire was up I fetched a towel and started to dry her hair. I took my time. I looked at her scalp and I thought, this is the head of the woman I love, the mother of my child. She put her head in my lap and lay down in front of the fire, and when I looked again she had fallen asleep.

Contributors

Penny Anderson has written for the *NME,* and BBC radio, as well as worked as a record company talent scout, a body parts courier, and a filing clerk in a sewerage works. She is presently writing a novel.

Patrick Belshaw is a retired HM Inspector of Schools who has recently completed an MA in Creative Writing at Northumbria University. The author of 'A Kind of Private Magic', Deautsch, 1994 (a group biography featuring EM Forster), he is married to Kathie and has three sons and two grandsons.

Sheena Brabazon worked for several years as a magazine journalist before beginning an MA in Writing. Since then she has had a short story, 'Ciara's Bird', published in an online magazine, *E-Sheaf*, and is currently working on her first novel.

Jaime Campbell is currently working on his first novel 'Harmonica' whilst completing an MA in Writing at Manchester Metropolitan University. He has recently published work in *Word Riot* and *Open Wide*. 'The Removal' is set to be made into a short film early in 2005.

Tim Cooke has worked variously as a lecturer, an internet consultant, and a composer of music for television, film and new media. His unpublished novel 'The Zero-Sum Game' was the source for the 2004 film 'The Principles of Lust' directed by Penny Woolcock. He lives (with a headache) in Manchester.

Penny Feeny is a former copywriter and editor now concentrating on fiction. Her short stories have been published in literary magazines and anthologies and won prizes in several competitions. She lives in Liverpool with her family.

Sara Heitlinger grew up in Australia and Israel. She has an MA in Creative Writing from the University of East Anglia. She won first prize in the *Time Out* Student Awards in 2003 for her short story, 'Empty'.

Philip Hughes was born in Birmingham, is 22 years old and is presently living in Aberystwyth where he studied English and Media. Having since completed a Masters in Creative Writing he is now working on a first novel in his spare time.

Annie Kirby is a graduate of the University of East Anglia Creative Writing MA. Her first short story was recently broadcast on Radio 4 as part of their 'Ones to Watch' series. She lives in Dorset.

David Lambert was born in the West Indies of Trinidadian/Irish parentage. He has an MA in Creative Writing from UEA. His unpublished novel 'Mulatto Moon' was a National Black First Chapter winner (2004). His novella 'Providence' won the Norwich Prize (2002). He is currently working on something set in the former Soviet Union. He teaches Creative Writing in Cambridge.

Zoe Lambert has an MA in Creative Writing from the University of East Anglia and is finishing her first novel. She writes reviews for various magazines. She is an associate lecturer and PhD student at Manchester Metropolitan University.

Char March has written three collections of poetry, most recently *Deadly Sensitive* (Grassroots Press), five BBC Radio 4 plays and six stage plays. She grew up in Scotland and now divides her time between the Highlands and Yorkshire.

Adam Maxwell is 28 years old and has been writing short-short stories or 'flash fiction' for his website (www.jigsawlounge.co.uk) and others for some time. He is currently working on his first novel. This piece is based on a true story.

Rory Miller wrote his contribution for a Creative Writing module as an undergraduate at the University of Kent, under the tutelage of Susan Wicks. He is presently living in Canada.

Tom Palmer works for the Reading Agency and as a freelance Reader Development Officer for Yorkshire and the North West. He has previously published *If You're Proud to be a Leeds Fan* (Mainstream, 2002). This story is loosely drawn from a novel in progress titled 'News Junkie', for which he received a K Blundell Award for development.

Mario Petrucci has been resident poet at the Imperial War Museum and with BBC Radio 3. He recently won the London Writers Competition for an unprecendented third time. 'Heavy Water' (Enitharmon) secured the Arvon Prize.

Fiona Ritchie Walker's first poetry collection, *Lip Reading*, was published by Diamond Twig in 1999. She has a second, *Garibaldi's Legs*, due from Iron Press in 2005. She received a 2004 Northern Promise Award from New Writing North to develop her short stories, and is presently working with Sara Maitland as part of NWN's mentoring scheme.

Maria Roberts was born in 1977 in Manchester. She studied English and Spanish at the University of Manchester and has just graduated from the Creative Writing School at MMU. She lives in a small house full of junk on the outskirts of Manchester with Scratch, her very talkative six-year-old son. She has just completed her first novel.

Sarah Tierney is 27, works as a journalist and copywriter, and lives in Manchester.

Emma Unsworth is 25 and works as a writer and editor. She began her first novel whilst studying for an MA in Creative Writing at Manchester University. Previous short stories have been published in *Comma: an anthology* and *September Stories* published by Prospect magazine and Comma Press.

Acknowledgements

Special thanks to City Shorts editors Angela Readman, Isaac Shaffer and Tane Vayu; in particular to Comma's co-founder Sarah Eyre, who worked tirelessly on the enormous selection process behind this project. Comma Press has benefited from the financial support of Arts Council England, and the personal assistance of Bron Williams, Avril Heffernan, Kate Griffin and Rachael Ogden. Comma has also been assisted by the Index Publishing Network Northwest and, through it, the Creative Industry Development Service (CIDS) in Manchester. For his encouragement and enthusiasm in particular, Comma would like to thank Dale Hicks. Credit is also due to Steven Waling for his close reading on affiliated projects, Claire Malcolm and Rachel Felberg for their encouragement, and Neil Porter for his keen eye.

]